EIGHT
PRINCESSES
AND A MAGIC MIRROR

For information about permission to reproduce selections from this book,
write to Permissions, W. W. Norton & Company, Inc.,
500 Fifth Avenue, New York, NY 10110

For information about special discounts for bulk purchases,
please contact W. W. Norton Special Sales at
specialsales@wwnorton.com or 800-233-4830

Manufacturing by Toppan Leefung
Book design by Jessie Price

Library of Congress Cataloging-in-Publication Data

Names: Farrant, Natasha, author. | Corry, Lydia, illustrator.
Title: Eight princesses and a magic mirror / Natasha Farrant ;
illustrated by Lydia Corry.
Description: First American edition. | New York, NY : Norton Young Readers,
[2020] | Audience: Ages 8-12. | Summary: A magic mirror reveals itself to
diverse princesses when each needs it most, illuminating how their power
comes not from titles or beauty, but from inner strength.
Identifiers: LCCN 2019049687 | ISBN 9781324015567 (cloth) |
ISBN 9781324015574 (epub)
Subjects: CYAC: Princesses—Fiction. | Short stories.
Classification: LCC PZ7.F2406 Eig 2020 | DDC [Fic]—dc23
LC record available at https://lccn.loc.gov/2019049687

W. W. Norton & Company, Inc. 500 Fifth Avenue, New York, N.Y. 10110
www.wwnorton.com

W. W. Norton & Company Ltd., 15 Carlisle Street, London W1D 3BS

1 2 3 4 5 6 7 8 9 0

Eight princesses and a Magic Mirror

NATASHA FARRANT

illustrated by LYDIA CORRY

NORTON YOUNG READERS

An Imprint of W. W. Norton & Company · Independent Publishers Since 1923

For my princesses
—NF

For Sylvie, with
all my love
—LC

CONTENTS

THE ENCHANTRESS AND THE MAGIC MIRROR

O nce upon a time, in a faraway place, a king and a queen asked a powerful enchantress to be godmother to their baby daughter. The enchantress replied that she would be delighted and promised to help her goddaughter become an excellent princess.

But later, as she was getting ready for bed, the enchantress wondered what she had let herself in for.

"An excellent princess," she mused. "What does that actually mean?"

"It means," scolded a maid, as she tugged a brush through the enchantress's tangled hair, "that she must be pretty."

"And tidy," grumbled another maid, picking up the

clothes the enchantress had dropped on the floor.

"Hmm."

The enchantress jumped into bed and landed on the cat, who hissed that excellent princesses—unlike enchantresses—were always kind to animals.

Pretty, tidy, and kind to animals.

It wasn't enough.

Now, in the enchantress's library, hanging from floor to ceiling between two bookcases, was an ancient magic mirror, gold and engraved, which claimed to know the answer to every question in all the worlds. The enchantress didn't consult it often, because it was grumpy and full of its own importance, but it occurred to her that it might be able to help. She flung back her blankets and padded down the corridor to the library.

"What makes a princess excellent?" she asked.

The mirror was silent. The enchantress sighed.

"Mirror, mirror on the wall, wisest and best of mirrors all, what makes a princess excellent?"

Still the mirror did not speak.

"What *now*?" cried the enchantress. "I asked you properly, didn't I?"

"It's not an easy question," said the mirror.

"But you're supposed to know everything!"

"Clean fingernails," said the mirror. "And being good at lessons."

The enchantress groaned.

"Also, manners," the mirror added.

The enchantress went back to bed.

    ᘓ * ᘓ

All night, the enchantress tossed and turned. She fell asleep just before dawn but woke around teatime with a plan.

"What we need," she told the mirror, "is to find out about other princesses. Lots of other princesses."

"That is the sort of question it takes a lifetime to answer," it informed her. "You have one month until your goddaughter's naming day, and you are very busy. *Too* busy, if you ask me, which you never do.

You'll just have to do the best you can for the child."

"Oh, I intend to."

The enchantress held out her hands, as if she were trying to frame the mirror between them.

"What are you doing?" it asked.

The enchantress smiled.

It happened fast. One moment the grand old mirror was in its rightful place in the enchanted palace. Then the air began to shimmer, and—*pfffff!*—the library had vanished, replaced by a forest. The mirror had shrunk to the size of a compact, the sort with a clasp that you flick open and that people keep in their pockets or handbags. It was still gold and engraved but—well—it was small.

"What have you done?" it cried.

"Shh," whispered the enchantress. "A princess is coming."

"Make me big again!"

But the enchantress was hanging the mirror from the branch of a tree on a scarlet ribbon.

"Be my eyes and ears in the universe," she whispered. "Know all who come across you."

THE
PRINCESS
AND THE
KNIGHTS

THE
PRINCESS
AND THE
KNIGHTS

Heart thumping, Princess Héloïse rode alone through the dark forest, on a quest to find a witch to save her poor sick sister, Emmeline. This was not, she felt, how things were supposed to be. Her father's castle was full of enormous knights with equally enormous horses. Knights armed to the teeth with swords and bows and arrows, and all highly experienced at questing. Héloïse excelled at studying but she was small and unarmed, had no sense of direction, and was riding a fat little pony called Snowflake.

Yet here she was.

Questing.

Not that she was surprised. Héloïse had a poor

opinion of the knights, who all wanted to marry Emmeline and spent their whole time showing off by fighting, jousting, and, lately, chopping down trees in the deep, dark forest to build grand castles. The forest grew back faster than they could chop it down, with ten trees growing for every one they felled, but they were too stupid to stop, or to realize that Emmeline didn't care about castles. All Emmeline cared about was poetry and eternal love. Despite the knights' showing off, when the castle doctor announced that he could not save poor Emmy, and Héloïse sensibly suggested that one of them should ride out to find the witch who lived in the deep, dark forest, they had dithered like chickens in a farmyard.

"But this witch is a gifted healer!" Héloïse cried.

"She turns people into pumpkins!" said one of the knights.

"Toads!" declared another.

"She puts people into cages and fattens them up to eat!" whispered a third.

"We wouldn't be able to find her anyway," announced a fourth. "That's the way of witches. They play tricks with the forest until you're lost and then *they* find you."

"I don't believe any of you are strong *or* brave," grumbled Héloïse.

She pulled on her cloak, swapped her velvet slippers for boots, and, after tying a piece of string around her glasses in case she fell off, trotted away on Snowflake.

It did not take her long to realize that the fourth knight had been right: the witch was playing tricks with the forest.

Héloïse had set out on a wide, straight path. But when she glanced back to see how far she'd come, the path was gone, replaced by a thick, close line of

trees. She looked ahead: there it was, stretching out before her. She nudged Snowflake on, then stopped and looked back.

Gone again.

The trees pressed toward her, their branches like a skeleton's hand.

Héloïse's heart thundered.

Pumpkins . . .

Toads . . .

Cages, fattening up and eating . . .

Perhaps if she charged, the trees would let her through.

She kicked Snowflake, bouncing in the saddle until her glasses slipped down her nose.

"Gee up!"

Snowflake didn't budge, and the trees crept closer. . . . Héloïse sighed.

"You're right. We have to go on, for Emmy."

She pushed her glasses back up her nose and rode deeper and deeper into the darker and darker forest with the trees always close behind until, suddenly, the path ended.

She was in a clearing full of sunlight and birdsong. In the middle, surrounded by a neat herb garden, was a cottage, its windows framed by a tumble of pink roses. A very small old woman stood by the garden gate, a raven on her shoulder and a fox cub at her feet.

She appeared to be casting a spell.

Héloïse had found the witch.

ᓚ * ᓚ

Héloïse wasn't sure what she had expected in a witch, but it certainly wasn't this.

"Why, 'tis a child, like you," the old woman crooned to the fox cub. "And there was I expecting one of them pesky tree-chopping knights."

Héloïse slid off Snowflake's back and dropped into a wobbly curtsy.

"If you please, ma'am . . . I am the Princess Héloïse and I have come to ask if you would kindly . . . "

Her voice caught, and she ended in a rush. "Please, my sister's ill, and the doctor says she'll die, and even though my father the king doesn't know I'm here, I'm sure he will pay however much gold you ask, and the knights wouldn't help even though they say they love her, but can you?"

The witch's eyes were quick and clever. "I don't want your father's gold. I want payment of a different kind, and I've a feeling in my bones I want it from you. Do you promise to pay, to save your sister?"

Pumpkins! thought Héloïse. *Toads! Cages and tricks! And now bones!*

But Emmeline . . .

"I promise."

"Then let's be away."

The witch clapped her hands twice, and a new path opened. She clapped again, and a bay mare appeared.

They rode out of the clearing together, the witch on the mare, with the raven flying overhead and the fox cub running alongside, Héloïse following on Snowflake. A few yards along the path, they saw a shiny object dangling by a scarlet ribbon from a branch.

"A mirror!" exclaimed Héloïse. "Whatever is that doing here?"

She reached for it, but the witch was quicker.

"Interesting," said the witch, and slid the mirror into one of her cloak's many pockets.

꙳ * ꙳

All the way to the castle, the witch talked. Héloïse's head spun. The witch knew so much!

She pointed out mushrooms that could kill at the smallest bite, and plants that could heal any wound, moths that looked like bark, and birds that looked like moths, vines that shot up overnight, and trees that were centuries old. Héloïse felt that she had never properly looked at the world before, and now she saw that the forest was like a glorious, living library.

Héloïse *loved* libraries.

After riding a while they stopped by some newly felled trees. Héloïse gasped. The forest looked like a graveyard. There must be four dozen trees cut down, all ancient.

The witch and her mare were still as the fallen trunks. Not a flick nor a twitch from either of them. Only the witch's cloak moved, and as it fluttered about her it sounded like the rustle of leaves.

At last, she gave a shuddering breath.

"Come," she said. "Your sister waits."

Héloïse looked over her shoulder as they rode away. A copse of young trees was growing, already tall and strong, where the old trees had fallen. She glanced at the witch.

She seemed smaller—more stooped.

"It is tiring work," said the witch, reading her mind.

For the first time, it occurred to Héloïse that by bringing her to Emmeline, she might be putting the witch in danger.

"There are knights," she said. "In the castle. They hate you. I'm afraid they want to kill you."

Sure enough, as they entered the Great Hall, the knights rose as one with their hands on their swords. But before they could take a step toward the witch a cloud of seeds and dandelion puffs from nowhere blew straight into their eyes.

"Witchcraft!" bellowed the blinded knights. "Kill her!"

"Feed her to the rats!"

"Hang her by the ankles!"

But by the time they could see again, the witch and Héloïse were gone.

In Emmeline's chamber, the witch built up the fire and boiled a cauldron of water. She measured in herbs drawn from the deep pockets of her cloak and made a potion. Emmeline drank every drop, then fell back onto her pillow, white as morning snow.

"She's dead!" wailed the maid who had been tending the fire.

She's dead! She's dead! She's dead! The cry echoed to the Great Hall, and the castle shook under the weight of the knights' boots as they thundered up the stairs.

"Give us the witch!"

Swords at the ready, they threw open the door to Emmeline's chamber. . . .

Héloïse gasped as a hawthorn hedge sprang up to bar their way. She looked fearfully at the witch.

"Oh, witch!" she whispered. "Have you killed my sister?"

"Hush your worrying, Princess, and pay no heed to those ruffians. Have an eye to your sister instead."

Héloïse obeyed. Was she imagining it, or was pink returning to Emmeline's cheeks?

Her heart danced.

"She's *sleeping*!" she shouted through the hawthorn hedge. "Go away!"

The knights slunk back downstairs to the sound of Héloïse's laughter.

For three days and three nights, sitting at her sister's bedside waiting for her to wake, Héloïse plied the witch with questions. What was in the potion she had given Emmy? What would she give the princesses' maid for her headaches? Or their father for his aching joints?

"Elderberry and yarrow," the witch murmured. "Valerian and red raspberry, feverfew, willow bark, meadow saffron and heather . . . "

"What would you do if a knight were wounded in battle?"

"Leave him to die, probably," cackled the witch, and Héloïse petted the fox cub to hide her grin.

"Could you make an eternal love potion?" she asked. "Emmy would like that, when she wakes up. It's all she ever thinks about."

"Eternal love!" The witch tapped her fingertips together. "Now that is more difficult. . . . For eternal love, you need the single star flower with solid gold tips that grows at the summit of the tallest of the Eastern Mountains, and a scale of the emerald fire dragon that protects it...."

Héloïse's eyes grew round as plums. "*Dragons exist?*"

The witch laughed. Héloïse blushed.

"Now don't look like that, Princess, all crestfallen and embarrassed. You're not the first to ask, and you won't be the last. I'm not saying dragons don't exist, but there's no such thing as a flower with solid gold tips. And even if there were, love's not something you can drink. Love is courage, and kindness, and a whole lot of other things besides ... like riding through a tricksome forest for your sister and sitting with her till she's better. You didn't need to pick a flower for that, did you?"

Héloïse felt a little better. "Can I learn?" she asked. "About plants and healing? Could I do it too, or do you have to be magic?"

"You've brains, haven't you, and courage? Why shouldn't you learn, when all this is over?"

"You mean when Emmy's better?"

"That too," said the witch.

The witch, in the castle! The knights couldn't believe their luck. You would think they would be grateful that Emmy was better, but they weren't. The witch and Héloïse had shown what cowards they were, and they couldn't forgive that. And something else . . .

The way those seeds and puffs had blown into their eyes . . .

The way that hawthorn hedge had appeared . . .

"She's the one who's been spoiling our castles!" realized one of the less stupid knights. "I'll bet she poisoned Princess Emmeline too. With a spell! Then came along to save her, to impress the king!"

"Kill her!"

"Avenge our honor!"

"Save our castles!"

The king wouldn't like it, of course, because he thought the witch had saved Emmeline. But that was too bad.

The witch, in the castle!

On the morning of the fourth day, Emmeline woke up and asked for breakfast. With a wave of the witch's hand, the hawthorn hedge disappeared, and Héloïse ran to the kitchen. When she returned, she found her sister's chamber in an uproar, full of knights shouting, and Emmeline crying, and the king pacing back and forth. The witch stood perfectly still and quiet in the middle of it all, wrapped in her traveling cloak, just as she had been when Héloïse first saw her. And when the king gave in and the knights marched the witch away, it seemed to Héloïse that she glided through the castle as easily as she had ridden through the forest, with the raven on her shoulder and the fox cub at her feet, and her cloak rustling like leaves.

Down they took her, down, down to the deepest cell in the damp, dire dungeon.

"Let's see her get out of that!" they roared as they locked the spiked iron door.

In the Great Hall, Héloïse begged for the witch to be released. The knights accused her of poisoning and treason.

"Kill the witch!"

"Let her live!"

"She poisoned the princess!"

"She saved Emmy's life!"

On and on they shouted, with no

sign of ever stopping, when . . .

CRACK!

A giant oak tree exploded through the floor and . . .

SMASH!

The stained-glass window above the stairs shattered as ivy burst through the panes.

A guard ran in, shouting, "The witch has escaped!"

Willow shoots sprang up between the flagstones.

"What's happening?" wailed the king.

"'Tis the witch!" shouted the knights. "She will destroy your castle, sire, as she has destroyed ours!"

And then silence fell, because into the commotion trotted the fox cub and flew the raven with something

shiny in their jaw and beak, which they dropped like gifts at Héloïse's feet.

From the fox cub, she received the mirror the witch had plucked from the branch.

From the raven, a gold coin.

"What is the meaning of this?" cried the knights, as the ivy snaked around the pillars of the Great Hall.

"Héloïse, explain yourself!" stammered the king, as the fire in the grate blew out in a tumble of pink roses.

Héloïse picked up the coin and weighed it in one hand. "The witch wants payment," she said. She picked up the mirror. She did not say, "And I am the one who must pay," but went slowly up the stairs to her own

chamber, carpets of violets sprouting beneath her feet. She closed the door and sat on her window seat with the fox and the raven. She put the gold coin in her pocket and opened the mirror.

A small, pale princess peered back at her, with string tied to glasses that sat lopsided on her nose, and eyes tired from watching over a sick bed.

"I don't understand," she told the fox and the raven.

She snapped the mirror shut and dropped it onto the window seat. Wild strawberries spread around it. She glared at them. She heard footsteps, Emmy's door opening, and her sister shouting that there were *hazel trees* growing in her room.

The fox nosed the mirror back toward her. She opened it again. What wasn't she seeing?

There she was, small and . . . Héloïse looked closer. It *was* her in the mirror, but somehow she *didn't* look small. She raised her chin. What was it the witch had said to her? *You've brains and courage, haven't you?* She straightened her glasses, raised her chin still further— she *had* been brave, and she knew she was clever. . . .

The fox yapped. She glanced at him. He stretched

his snout toward the strawberries. The raven tilted her head.

"I don't *understand*," Héloïse said.

In among the strawberries, a single star flower appeared then vanished, its petals tipped with gold.

"Oh!" gasped Héloïse. "*Oh!*"

The raven pecked her ear. The fox licked her chin.

Héloïse jumped down from the window seat and ran to find her sister.

ᴄᴜᴅ ✳ ᴄᴜᴅ

"A quest!" announced the king. "A quest for a chance to win the hand of the fair Emmeline!

"On the summit of the tallest of the Eastern Mountains, protected by the emerald fire dragon, grows a single star flower, its petals tipped with solid gold. Whosoever brings back this flower and a scale from the dragon's back shall win my daughter's eternal love, and marry her, and, on my death, become king!"

By sundown, all the knights were gone. And, of course, since the star flower did not exist, none of them ever found it. They were so embarrassed that they never returned. The witch was never seen again either, though the forest continued to grow back whenever anyone tried to chop it down, so Héloïse guessed she was still in her cottage, doing her work. The king and his family repaired the broken windows of their castle and rebuilt the walls, but there wasn't much they could do about the oak tree in the Great Hall, or the flowers or willows or hazel trees. So they kept them, and soon the castle became famous for being the only one in the world to have a forest inside it as well as out.

Emmeline married a poet who loved her forever. The king took up gardening as a hobby. As for Héloïse, she studied hard and became a powerful healer, just as the witch had told her she could, and people came from far and wide to learn from her.

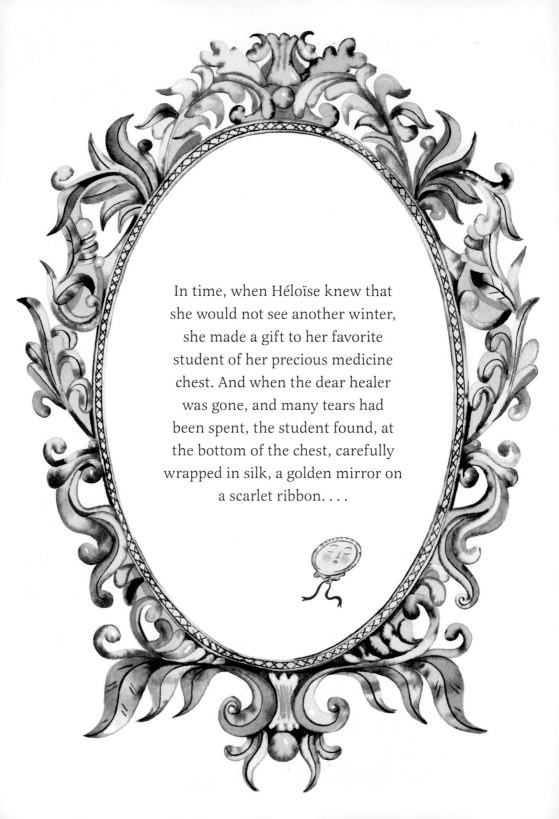

In time, when Héloïse knew that
she would not see another winter,
she made a gift to her favorite
student of her precious medicine
chest. And when the dear healer
was gone, and many tears had
been spent, the student found, at
the bottom of the chest, carefully
wrapped in silk, a golden mirror on
a scarlet ribbon. . . .

THE
DESERT
PRINCESS

THE DESERT PRINCESS

Silent as a panther, Princess Leila al'Aqbar crept through the dark courtyards of the Garden Palace. She stopped at the foot of a stout vine, checked to make sure no one was following then, one hand over the other, feet braced against the marble wall, began to climb. She paused on the parapet, head tilted to listen, one foot dangling into the void, the other hovering above the tiles of the Jasmine Terrace. It was a twenty-foot drop into the courtyard, but she wasn't afraid. She'd done this scores of times—hundreds of times! Had even boasted that she could do it blindfolded, though so far no one had dared her to, not even Hisham, who was waiting below for the all-clear.

Ah, but it was wonderful up here! Soon she must do what she was sworn to, fulfill Hisham's latest, maddest dare, and let loose all manner of mayhem. But for a moment she was alone between the stars and the desert. Beyond the walls of the palace compound, in the dunes rippling beneath the crescent moon, the fennec vixen that Leila had been watching for weeks was leading her cubs out to hunt. In the palace kitchens, servants were clearing dinner, while others carried trays of tea and pastries up to this very terrace. Horses, including her own silver Blaze, were snuffling at their hay nets in the stables. And she, Leila, was above it all! No longer a twelve-year-old girl, often grubby and usually in trouble, but a queen like her mother, mistress of all she surveyed. She stretched up her hand. If she reached high enough, she might even pluck a star. . . .

A shake of the vine informed her that Hisham had grown bored of waiting and was climbing up to join her.

Queen Leila of the Sands and Stars was banished, replaced by Princess Leila, Maker of Mischief. She grinned at Hisham as he joined her astride the parapet, his dark eyes dancing like hers.

"Ready?" he whispered.

Leila patted the cloth bag she wore across her body.

The bag wriggled in protest.

The roof terrace was covered by a pergola, thick with jasmine and climbing roses, a ceiling of flowers. Leila slept here sometimes in high summer when the nights were hot, waking as dawn broke pink and blue over the Western Mountains. It was her favorite part of the palace, but now it was being used by Queen Rania to entertain her guests. In flickering candlelight they sat at low tables, nibbling pastries, sipping tea and talking.

Always, *always*, talking . . .

When Leila was queen, she was not going to waste her time chatting. When Leila was queen, she would make her

guests spend their days galloping over sand dunes, hunting with falcons, and in the evenings maybe singing, like the desert nomads. When Leila was queen, she frequently informed her mother, nobody would be bored.

"Which goes to show you understand nothing about being queen," her mother typically replied, when she wasn't too busy reading or writing or giving orders.

All the kings of the desert were here this evening except for one, and they were talking about him. Snatches of conversation floated over the terrace.

"*Aziz is on the move . . . heavily armed . . . his black and gold colors are everywhere . . . soldiers, modern ideas, no respect for the old ways . . . we must invite him to talk . . .*"

This last comment from Rania, obviously. Leila rolled her eyes and nodded to Hisham.

Light as cats, they scurried along the edge of the wall. Still in darkness but level with the candlelight, they jumped softly back onto the parapet, then inched forward along the pergola until they were directly above the kings and Queen Rania. Hisham squeaked

as a rose thorn pierced his thumb. Leila glared.

They held their breath, but nobody looked up.

Leila felt a twinge of remorse at what she was about to do. Her mother sat below her, a queen among six kings. All were dressed in white, as was the custom on these occasions, but in Leila's eyes, Rania, in her close-fitting coat and billowing trousers, shone the brightest. The kings were arguing. Rania silenced them with a graceful flick of a jeweled finger; Leila felt a thrill of pride in her and hesitated.

But Hisham, flat on the strut across from her, was

making faces, and yesterday Leila had lost a dare over that whole messy business of wading through the eel mud in the lake, and honor must be saved. She wriggled until she was right above fat old King Amir.

A jasmine flower floated toward the table and landed in Queen Rania's glass.

Please don't look up! Oh, please! begged Leila silently.

Rania tilted her head. . . .

"I cannot agree!" Everyone jumped, including the spies in the pergola, as King Omar thumped the table. "Aziz is not to be trusted!"

Rania's attention returned to the table. Leila breathed again and, before she could lose her nerve, reached carefully into her cloth bag.

It is not easy to catch hold of a mouse, even when the mouse is imprisoned in a bag and cannot escape. Twice, Leila's fingers closed around its small furry body. Twice, it twisted away. Once, it bit her, and she had to clamp her lips together not to cry out. But eventually she got a firm hold of it, pulled it out of the bag—and let go. . . .

In their wildest dreams, Leila and Hisham could not have hoped for what happened next!

The mouse landed on King Amir's gleaming bald

head, bounced, then shot into his robes to hide.

Amir yelped and leaped to his feet, upsetting the table. A teapot fell into the lap of King Bruhier, who screamed, jumped up, and slipped on a tray of pastries. A palace cat, attracted by the commotion, slunk from the shadows and pounced on the mouse as it emerged from Amir's robes, tripping King Sami as he helped Bruhier to his feet. All the while Amir hopped about shrieking, "Get it away from me! Get it away from me!" and everyone else ran around shouting, "To arms! To arms! Aziz has attacked!" In the pergola above, helpless with laughter, Leila and Hisham crept away.

Back at the parapet, there remained a final part of the dare to complete. Leila threw back her head and opened her mouth.

"*Ululululululu!*"

A battle cry, learned from Hisham, who had it from a cousin who had traveled

beyond the mountains and fought in real wars. Leila loved the way it vibrated from her throat to her toes, the way it made her feel bigger and taller. She could see herself, standing in her stirrups as Blaze galloped across the desert, the wind in her hair, sunlight glinting off the blade of her raised saber. . . .

How brave she was! How gallant! How . . .

"Got you!"

The arms of a palace guard closed around her. Leila's battle cry ended in a squeak.

ᘯ ＊ ᘯ

Leila, locked in her room, lay on her bed and fumed as she relived her mother's scolding.

"*When will you learn that you are a princess not a desert urchin . . . screaming like a savage . . . this was an important meeting, we were not gathered to*

play but to discuss the grave danger that threatens the kingdoms . . . I'm embarrassed, Leila, embarrassed and ashamed. . . . "

Throughout the Battle of the Jasmine Terrace, one person had not moved. Queen Rania had not run, or shouted or shrieked or screamed, and she most certainly had not stepped in pastries or upset teapots. Just narrowed her eyes at the quivering shadows retreating along the rafters and nodded to her guards.

It had been the same lecture as always, but this time with six kings, watching and tutting and muttering—and Rania's final order to *take a good look at yourself in the mirror, young lady, and decide what you want to become.*

Leila had no time for mirrors. There was only one in her room, a compact on a scarlet ribbon, a present, before he had died, from her father. . . . She snapped it open now and glared at it. Her reflection glared back, dirty and bedraggled, with twigs of jasmine in her hair.

I'm ashamed of you.

If only her mother could see her, just once, as she saw herself! Saber in hand, standing in her stirrups, galloping across the dunes with the wind in her hair! Or quiet

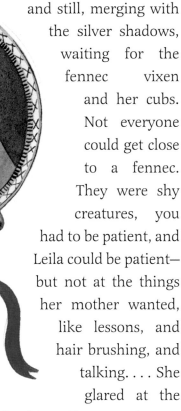

and still, merging with the silver shadows, waiting for the fennec vixen and her cubs. Not everyone could get close to a fennec. They were shy creatures, you had to be patient, and Leila could be patient— but not at the things her mother wanted, like lessons, and hair brushing, and talking. . . . She glared at the mirror again. It was . . . oddly shiny. She peered more closely. No, nothing was different, except . . . She raised her chin, swept back her hair, gazed down her nose, and flared her nostrils as Rania did when she gave a command.

Leila had inherited her father's dark eyes, his smile, even his dimples. She had never realized, before, how much she also looked like her mother.

She didn't suppose her mother had ever noticed either. Or that she would care, even if she had. She stuffed the mirror into the pocket of her coat and rolled off the bed over to the window.

She leaned out of the open window and thought she heard her father's voice. *One day, little one, we will ride out to watch the dawn together from the Western Mountains. You will see then how big the world can be.*

Oh, Papa!

Oh, the silver rippling dunes, the endless desert, the moon! Blaze in his stable, his breath on her neck when he greeted her, the soft pounding of his hooves on the sand! The vixen and her cubs, the pink and blue of sunrise! What was she still doing here? The locked door was a joke. How many times had she sneaked out through the window, slunk from the palace into the desert? She listened—no voices, now, no footsteps. The night, still as still, everyone asleep but her. . . .

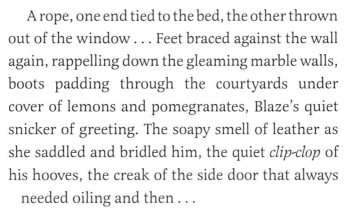

A rope, one end tied to the bed, the other thrown out of the window ... Feet braced against the wall again, rappelling down the gleaming marble walls, boots padding through the courtyards under cover of lemons and pomegranates, Blaze's quiet snicker of greeting. The soapy smell of leather as she saddled and bridled him, the quiet *clip-clop* of his hooves, the creak of the side door that always needed oiling and then ...

Freedom!

A short trot to warm up, a slow canter, a whooping gallop, and not a king or queen in sight. Just a princess and her horse riding beneath the stars, on and on until they reached the foothills of the Western Mountains.

ᗑ * ᗑ

Leila slid off Blaze's back, kissed his nose, then leaned against him while they both caught their breath. A shooting star traced a bright path across the sky, and she closed her eyes tight, only opening them when she had made her wish.

"We're going to go on like this forever," she whispered to Blaze. "We're never going back. We'll carry on up into the mountains where the whole world is green, then down to the sea where we'll gallop through the waves. We'll become famous, like a story. People will write books about us!"

Blaze snorted.

It was a small sound in all that desert.

There were snakes out here, scorpions and sandstorms. Leila had ridden this far before, but never alone. She had sneaked out on her own, but never this far. . . . She shivered. Not because she was scared, she told herself, or because if something happened to her, nobody would know where she was. It was just that the wind had picked up, and that desert nights are cold, and she felt tired after her ride.

She reached into her saddlebag for a blanket and her water bottle, found a handful of almonds that she shared with Blaze. She drew comfort from the warmth, the drink and food, her horse snuffling the nuts from her hand. He rested his head on her shoulder, and she slid her arm around his neck and turned her face to the stars.

Once, her tutor had told her that the stars could sing

(it was the only time she had almost liked him). She hadn't believed him, of course, but with no Hisham to laugh at her, it was worth a try. . . . Feeling slightly foolish, she cupped her hands over her ears.

And froze.

She could hear singing!

Except, would the stars sing with human voices?

And did the stars laugh?

Because there was laughter, as well as music, borne toward Leila on the westerly wind. Blaze pricked his ears. Could horses hear stars?

Leila didn't think so.

"Let's go and look."

Leila crept through the shadows of the foothills, leading Blaze. The singing grew louder. She came to a ridge, and saw flickering firelight . . . a camp, with hundreds of men. Flags fluttered over their tents, black and gold, reminding her of something, but what? The singing came from a group of men sitting around one of the fires. Leila craned forward to hear better, then shrank back as a man emerged from the tent closest to her.

He was younger than many of the men, and he was dressed like them in a padded black coat over

loose black trousers tucked into boots, but he had the assured, confident bearing of a prince.

No, not a prince—a king!

A king who rode under a banner of black and gold . . .

A king with soldiers, on the move . . .

A king who had not been at the Garden Palace . . .

Leila never rode as hard as she rode that night. "I'm

sorry, old friend," she whispered to Blaze as she urged him into a gallop back home. Blaze was exhausted, but as if he understood that everything depended on him, he never slowed. On and on he galloped, through the chill desert night, hooves pounding the sand, until sweat poured from horse and girl.

As the Garden Palace gleamed into view in the pink and blue of dawn, Leila stood in her stirrups, threw back her head, and screamed.

"*Ululululululu!*"

꙳ ✳ ꙳

When Aziz's men attacked, the Garden Palace was ready for them. The battle was brutal but short. Rania, watching from the Jasmine Terrace with the kings, saw how evenly matched the two sides were. She understood that unless she intervened, it would not stop until too many were dead. And so she sent a messenger to parley with Aziz, and the queen and all the kings talked through the day and into the following

night, and for many more days and many more nights after that, until a peace was agreed, and a new order was born, which included some of Aziz's modern ideas, and some of the desert's old ways. Everyone agreed it would not have been possible if Leila, the quick-as-a-panther, desert-urchin princess had not ridden like the wind to warn her mother of what was coming. And as Leila raised her chin and smiled proudly, she did not need a mirror to tell her that she looked, if not like a queen, at least like a queen in waiting.

Which was just as well, because the
mirror had long fallen from her
pocket, and was lying in the sand,
waiting for someone to find it. . . .

THE
PRINCESS
OF ABSOLUTE
LOVELINESS

THE PRINCESS OF ABSOLUTE LOVELINESS

High on the tallest of the Central Mountains nestles the ancient city of Bamfou. Forest stretches into the clouds above it, and far below, sea the color of sapphires glitters and breaks on dark beaches. But it is the river that flows around the city in lazy loops that allows it to thrive. The people of Bamfou have planted gardens on its banks, where they grow rice and yams and okra, coffee and berries and melon. Legend says the river is guarded by a shaman who lives in the forest, a wise woman over a thousand years old. For the most part, she does an excellent job of keeping the water flowing pure and sweet, never too slow nor too fast. Every few years, when the rains come, and the river bursts its

banks, the townspeople grumble that she must have fallen asleep. Then the sun comes out again and they forget.

The city is built of white stone, with leafy squares where people sit at café tables playing cards. The air is full of the smell of rich cooking, of talk and music. On the second biggest square is the market where traders meet from far and wide. And in the biggest square of all is the palace, built of the same gleaming white stone as the rest of the city. Peacocks strut about its walls and guards in bright uniforms stand outside its golden gates. This may sound grand, but it is a friendly palace. The city's elders, when they are not playing cards in cafés, like to sit on the benches in the courtyard to swap stories about the old days, and on holidays, families bring picnics where children, including Princess Abayome, run about and play. Everyone loves Abayome because she never gives herself airs but is easy and generous and cheerful. Last year, a little girl called Odé was swept down from the forest in a flood that drowned her entire village, and now she sleeps in the princess's bedroom, and Abayome loves her like a sister.

That is the kind of place Bamfou is. Happy and kind and welcoming.

Or at least it was, until the king brought home his new queen.

ᕼ * ᕼ

Abayome was planting daisies in the palace flower beds with Odé when the king returned with his retinue. She had missed her father in the long months that he had been away. As soon as she heard the horses, she ran to greet him with Odé in her muddy gardening clothes.

"Father!"

"Daughter!"

Something was wrong. Instead of swinging Abayome around as he always did and then pressing her to his heart, the king turned, and in a voice trembling with love, said, "Abayome, my daughter, there is someone I want you to meet."

And he rushed forward to help a lady from her carriage.

Abayome's eyes widened. She had never seen a person so beautiful.

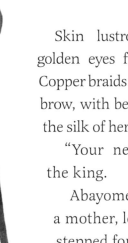

Skin lustrous as polished ebony, golden eyes fringed with long lashes. Copper braids woven around a high clear brow, with beads of turquoise to match the silk of her embroidered dress.

"Your new mother," murmured the king.

Abayome, who had not expected a mother, let alone one so splendid, stepped forward in a daze and only just remembered to bow.

"Goodness," the new queen said. "How dirty you are. Please do not come near me until you are clean."

Odé stared at Abayome, as if to say, *Really? You're going to let her talk to you like that?* and Abayome herself stared at her father with much the same astonishment.

But the king only had eyes for the queen.

And so everything changed.

ᴄ◡) ∗ ᴄ◡

On the evening the new queen arrived, a welcome feast was thrown on the palace's loveliest terrace. The chirrup of crickets and the scent of tobacco flowers filled the warm night air. Guests sat on woven cushions on the ground, eating spiced rice served on banana leaves with roasted lamb and pepper sauce, toasting the king and his new queen with coconut water straight from the shell. And after dinner, once they had split the coconuts to scoop out the flesh inside, the king asked Odé to sing.

Odé rarely spoke, but she loved to sing, and her voice was sweet as a nightingale's. She sang songs she remembered from her village. Abayome's favorite was about a place right on the edge of the forest with the dark green tree world on one side and the open mountains on the other,
and in between, a
waterfall
tumbling
into a pool
so clear
people
said the old
shaman had
cast a spell over
it to keep it secret.
It was a wonderful song
but a terrible one too, because it was about all that Odé had lost. When she finished everyone was very quiet, caught in its magic and thoughts about the beauty and cruelty of the world.

"Well!" The new queen shattered the silence. "I can see I have work to do. Tomorrow, I shall send for *proper* musicians, as well as furniture and plates."

Everyone stared at the king then, as if to say, *Are you*

really going to let her say that? and still the king beamed at his new wife with love and pride. Abayome glared at the queen. The queen gazed coolly back.

Abayome looked away first.

⁐ ✳ ⁐

For as long as she could remember, Abayome had done the same thing every morning during the dry season. She jumped out of bed as soon as the first birds started to sing and ran to the river beach outside the palace grounds to swim with the town children before they went to school. Then she ran back to the palace and ate a huge breakfast of sweet mangoes and omelet in the kitchen, before racing upstairs to get dressed in her most comfortable clothes. Next came lessons with her tutor, who let her study exactly what she wanted, which was usually stories about the old days, and the forest, and the wild creatures who lived there.

On the day after the new queen's arrival, when Abayome ran out of her room, a pale young woman in a smart blue dress stepped into her path.

"I am the queen's personal maid," said the pale

young woman. "My name is Mademoiselle Amélie. Her Grace has sent me to look after you."

"Look after me?"

"To wash and dress you," said Mademoiselle Amélie. "In the correct fashion."

Abayome did not take well to being washed and dressed in the correct fashion. She howled as she was plunged into a tub of scalding water and squealed as her thick eyebrows were plucked to narrow lines. She whimpered as her nails were filed and she gagged as her skin was rubbed all over with lotions. When Amélie started tugging through her tangled hair, Abayome began to cry, then watched in silent horror as it was oiled then parted into dozens of braids secured with pink and white beads to match her new stiff, starched dress.

When it was over, Mademoiselle Amélie took her to the queen, who smiled and held out a small gold mirror. Abayome stared at her reflection.

"Is that me?" she breathed.

The queen smiled again. "You may keep the mirror."

The king was sent for.

"Are you not proud of her, my love?" asked the queen.

The king could have told the truth, which was that he was always proud of Abayome. But instead he said, "Oh, yes, my love—why, she is just like you."

Abayome had won the queen's approval. But she lost many things.

She lost Madu, the head gardener, who had taught her

about plants, and Fayola, her nursemaid, who still sang her to sleep, and Baba and Beji, the cooks, who slapped her hands when they caught her trying to steal cakes, then gave her the cakes anyway. They were her family, and she loved them.

But the queen said, "A princess does not mix with servants."

And so Abayome did not mix with servants.

The queen said, "A princess does not need to learn silly stories about the past, and the forest and its wild creatures. A princess's education is a serious affair."

And so Abayome did not protest when her tutor was dismissed and replaced by a young man called Monsieur Étienne who smacked her fingers with a ruler if she mixed up dates of wars and treaties.

The queen said, "A princess does not run wild with other children, and a princess does not swim in rivers."

And so Abayome lost her playmates and her greatest pleasure.

When the queen said, as they always knew that she would, "A princess does not share her room with an orphan child from the forest," even the king protested. But the queen was firm and Odé moved out of the palace and in with Madu and his family.

Abayome accepted this, like everything else, for love
of her father. But the next time she saw Odé, she
turned her head away in shame. And when she heard
that Odé had stopped singing, her shame grew.

On lonely evenings, when there were guests in the
castle and the queen would not allow her in the new
dining room, Abayome would look in the mirror for
comfort.

"Show me how beautiful I am," she would order,
and the mirror did.

She told herself that as long as she was beautiful,
she must also be loved.

Months passed. Inside the palace, Abayome grew
more elegant, more polished and glossy and groomed,
while outside the season turned. Every afternoon
more and more clouds drifted up from the sea. They
clung thickly to the forest and turned to rain that
dripped off leaves and spilled down rocks, formed
ponds and puddles and channels through the dark
earth. The channels gathered speed until they hurtled
into the river, churning it to a torrent that smashed
through banks and trees and pastures, growing
bigger and faster and unstoppable.

Everyone agreed, the shaman in the forest

must be sleeping deeply. These were the worst floods anyone could remember.

A tree whirled down the mountain and smashed into a bridge, cutting the town in two.

A cow was swept away, never to be seen again.

A garden collapsed, a family's livelihood destroyed.

And then Odé disappeared.

The head gardener Madu came to the palace to ask for guards to help with the search party.

"But why?" asked the queen. "I mean, what concern is Odé of ours?"

"My love!" protested the king.

"If you please, Your Grace," stammered Madu, "she is like a daughter to us—to the whole town. Like a *sister*."

He stared at Abayome, who felt her cheeks grow hot.

Alone in her room, she took out the mirror.

"Am I beautiful?" she whispered.

The mirror showed her a girl with thin eyebrows and polished skin and braided hair secured with colored beads.

Abayome began to cry. She cried until she was puffier and more pink and piggy-eyed than any princess ever was, and then she looked in the mirror again, to see what she had become, and saw to her surprise that the mirror had begun to shimmer.

At first, she thought it must be a trick of the light. She moved away from the window. Still it shimmered. She crossed the room and sat on Odé's old bed. The shimmer became a steady glow, until there was no mirror anymore, just light pouring from it. Abayome blinked as it grew brighter. When she looked again the glow had gone, and something else had replaced it.

An image of a waterfall tumbling into a pool on the

edge of the forest, with the open mountain on one side, and the dark green world of trees on the other.

Abayome blinked again. When she looked in the mirror, she saw only her own reflection, but it didn't matter. She knew exactly where Odé was.

⌣⌣ ✳ ⌣⌣

Abayome left immediately. She told no one where she was going. She knew they would try to stop her, and that they would think her mad if she told them about the mirror. The search party was working downstream, assuming Odé had been swept away. Abayome slipped out of the palace gardens straight to the riverbank and began to walk upstream. It was harder than she had imagined. The ground was slick with mud, and she had to pick her way carefully through debris flung up by the floodwater. She lost one shoe, then another. Slipped. Stood up, her pale pink dress soaked to the skin. She pushed her hair out of her eyes, streaking her cheeks with mud, and carried on.

Up she went, up and up. The terraced farmland dropped away, and she walked the vast open mountain, past grazing zebra and startled pheasants. Mosquitoes bit her. Thorns ripped her clothes. Her stomach rumbled, and her parched tongue swelled in her mouth, but at last, late in the afternoon, she reached the forest.

Somewhere in its dark green world, she heard the roar of a waterfall.

More walking, past trees now with trunks as wide as a house and vines as thick as a grown man's arm, following the sound of water until at last she came on it, and it was every bit as lovely as Odé had sung it, a foaming, thundering cascade. Abayome watched, mesmerized. She walked up to the water. Reached out to touch it and wondered how it would feel to be in the water . . .

Under the water . . .

To *be* the water . . .

She leaned over until she felt the spray of the waterfall on her cheek . . . *oh!*

Abayome clutched a vine to stop herself tipping into the pool.

Was this part of the shaman's enchantment? Was *this* how she kept the pool secret?

Abayome edged away until her back was wedged against a cliff and took a shaky breath.

A wild creature began to howl. . . .

The mirror was hanging on a ribbon around

her neck. She pulled it over her head and opened it.

"Show me Odé," she begged, as another creature screeched.

But there was no shimmering or vision. The mirror reflected only her face, covered in bites and scratches, and the cliff behind her, and . . . *oh!*

Halfway up the cliff was a ledge. And on the ledge . . .

On the ledge, a human foot. A human foot that, as Abayome began to climb, revealed itself to be attached to a human leg, curled under a little human girl's dress, attached to a little human girl's body, lying hunched and motionless on a bed of leaves.

Abayome's heart was pounding as she heaved herself onto the ledge. She was too late! She was too late, and Odé had died alone and frightened in the forest where her entire world had once been swept away, and it was Abayome's fault, because she had been more concerned with pleasing the queen and being a beautiful princess than with caring for Odé.

"Abi?"

And now there were ghosts here as well as wild creatures, and the ghosts knew who she was, and they were calling to her.

"Abi! *Abi!* You *came!*"

And it wasn't ghosts at all, but Odé, who was in her arms, and she wasn't dead, and the clouds above were bursting and the rain was pouring through the high canopy, but the girls didn't care, because it was dry on their ledge between the forest and the open mountain, and they had each other, and they were safe.

They stayed the whole night in the forest, cuddled close for warmth and, though the screeches and howls grew louder and closer, they weren't afraid because they had each other. In the morning when the sun broke and the rain stopped, they walked back down the mountain, and they sang all the way.

When the first houses of the city appeared, Abayome stopped.

"We should probably tidy ourselves up a bit," she said, and reached for the mirror around her neck.

But the mirror had gone.

"It doesn't matter," said Odé. "Everyone will be so happy to see you. They won't care what you look like. They never did."

And Abayome knew that she was right.

The news that Odé had returned and that the princess had rescued her spread around the flooded town like a tidal wave, and by the time the girls reached the palace gates a happy procession of townspeople walked with them, singing and dancing and telling each other, "*That* is a true princess of Bamfou." Abayome agreed. And when she was dry, and dressed in her comfortable old clothes, she informed her father the king and her stepmother the queen that from now on her sister Odé would be sleeping in her room once more, and that, come the dry season, she would be swimming again in the river. And for once the king looked not at his queen but at his daughter and agreed that it should be so.

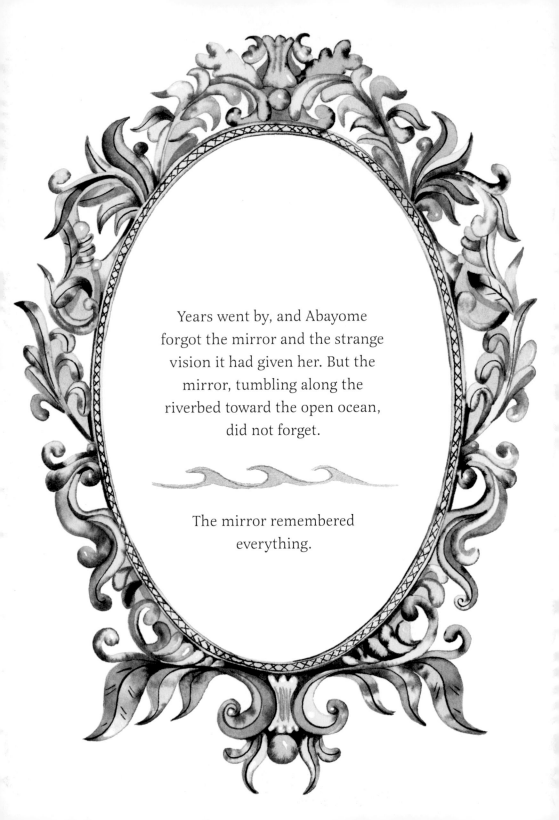

Years went by, and Abayome
forgot the mirror and the strange
vision it had given her. But the
mirror, tumbling along the
riverbed toward the open ocean,
did not forget.

The mirror remembered
everything.

THE
PRINCESS
OF THE
HIGH SEAS

THE PRINCESS OF THE HIGH SEAS

All the children on the island kingdom of Rhain were given their first boat on their twelfth birthday. It was one of those facts of life there, like midwinter bonfires and snowdrops in spring. The sight of the dories and cockles out in Taransay Bay on a clear, still day, their bright hulls reflected in the water, the excited young voices calling out across the waves, were a comforting reminder that island ways continued as they always had, and always would.

The only children not to receive a boat were the Rhainian princes and princesses. Boats for islanders are a matter of survival, for fishing and trade, but the sea is not always kind. Boats bring death too. The same

tradition that insisted that every island child *must* have a boat, also stated that the royal children must *not*. No one had ever questioned it, and at the time our story starts, three of the four princesses of Rhain were perfectly happy with this rule. Catriona, Ailsa, and Iseabail had no interest in going about on the water. It was not something princesses *did*. Princesses boarded boats only if they had to, for example, when they left to marry a prince, and when they did, someone else sailed them there, just as someone else always led their horses when they went out riding, and boiled water for their tea. A princess's job was to stay safe, doing

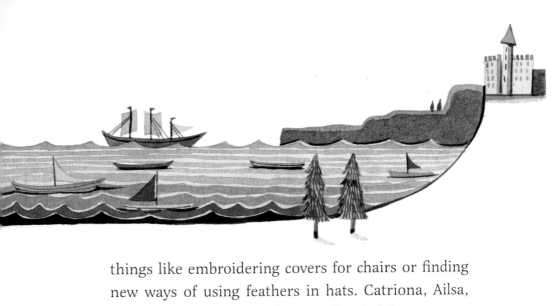

things like embroidering covers for chairs or finding new ways of using feathers in hats. Catriona, Ailsa, and Iseabail thought all this was delightful.

And then there was Ellen.

Ellen, unlike her older sisters, did not accept things just because they had always been so. Ellen questioned *everything*. Why must she sleep at night and wake by day? Why could she not wear clothes to run in instead of long skirts and petticoats? Or paddle on sunny days like the island children, or watch the Spring Regatta with the servants from the roof where everyone knew the view was best? It was no surprise to anyone when,

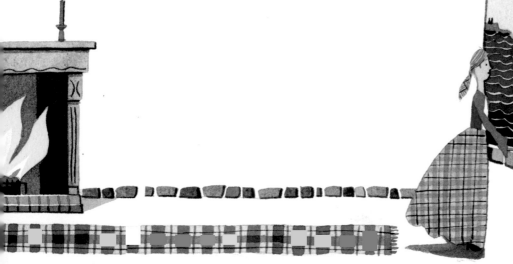

on her twelfth birthday, Ellen demanded, "Why may I not have a boat, like all the other children?"

The older princesses giggled. The king sighed. Only the queen said nothing.

"Because it has always been so," the king said, when he had finished sighing. "Try to be more like your sisters."

Ellen, who was not a *polite* kind of princess, said she didn't see why her father got to decide what she should do rather than letting her decide for herself, and she swept out of the breakfast room through the door to the servants' corridor. She stomped along a dark passage to the wine cellar, through another door, then ran and tumbled and stumbled down steep stone steps cut into the cliff until she reached the castle's quay, where she flung herself to the ground and burst into tears.

Of all the questions she had ever asked, this had been the most important, because Ellen loved the sea more than anything in the world. She had thought her parents understood.

She had hoped so much they would make an exception. . . .

Her tears spent, she sat with her knees drawn up to her chest, facing the waves. She wondered if anyone would recognize her if she chopped off all her hair and ran away to sea, or if it would be possible to steal a boat, or even secretly build one. She didn't hear her mother until the queen sat down beside her.

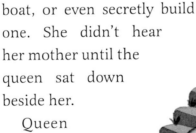

Queen Grizel was not from Rhain but from

Hean, where the rules are different and royals are let loose upon the water as soon as they are strong enough to pull an oar. She had been sorry to give up sailing when she married, and it pained her that her daughters would never know the same pleasure she had. As Catriona, Ailsa, and Iseabail's twelfth birthdays had come and gone, she had said nothing, because they had not. But, faced with Ellen's sorrow, she knew that she could keep quiet no longer.

"The sea has salt in it enough already, you know," she murmured. "So no more tears, youngling. Come away with me to Bhreac's shipyard, where only yesterday I saw a fine dory, an excellent beginner boat. We shall look at it together, and if you like it, it shall be yours."

Ellen caught her breath. Very, very slowly, she turned to gape at her mother. Grizel held out a hand.

"You are a child of Hean too, you know."

The day was gray and overcast, but Ellen's beam cut through the gloom like summer sun.

The dory was perfect, trim and compact, built for steadiness rather than speed. It would be a good teacher for a student who had everything to learn. Ellen's heart leaped with love the moment she saw it.

"But are you sure?" she whispered.

Her hands curled tight over the gunwale. She could not bear it if her mother changed her mind.

"Quite sure, my love," replied the queen. "So now there are only her colors left to choose, and her name. What will you have?"

Ellen chose light blue for the hull, to match the clear sky breaking through the clouds, with yellow sails and oar tips to match the sun. Shyly, she gave her mother the honor of choosing the boat's name.

Grizel frowned as she thought, then smiled.

"*Princess of the High Seas*," she said. "Painted in gold, for luck."

Princess of the High Seas. Ellen savored the roll of the words on her tongue.

The king was furious when he found out, and the islanders were shocked, but Grizel did not back down. She asked one thing of her daughter, that she would not go out beyond the calm waters of Taransay Bay. For a while, Ellen obeyed. But she was quick to learn, and the need to venture out of the sheltered harbor was like an itch. By midsummer, she was exploring neighboring coves. By August's end she was rowing

in and out of sea caves, pulling up to rest on hidden beaches or bobbing in pools formed by the tide, where seals and otters nosed about the hull and gulls perched on the *Princess*'s sides to preen. Ellen was brown as a nut, her hair bleached white from the salt and her limbs as lithe and tough as the coil of rope she kept for emergencies in the dory's watertight locker.

"No good will come of it," grumbled the king, and the other princesses agreed.

Queen Grizel did not scold Ellen for breaking her promise but waited for what she knew must happen.

∽ ✳ ∽

The storm came at the beginning of September.

It was the worst Rhain had seen in years. For two days, lightning ripped through thunderclouds, driving rain like bullets into the roaring sea. Inland, roads turned to streams, streams to rivers. No craft put out in such weather. Instead, islanders pulled their boats high onto the strand, then barred their doors and shutters, praying the damage would not be too great. In the castle, Ellen sat huddled by a turf fire in the watchtower. She loved the tower because it had windows on three sides overlooking the sea, and she could pretend she was in the crow's nest of one of the merchant schooners that sailed to Taransay on their voyages around the world.

It was her greatest wish to sail on such a ship.

On the third day, the storm eased. Weather vanes still spun in the unsettled wind, and the purple-blue of the waves warned of evil currents, but cottage doors opened and the islanders inspected the damage. There were roofs to mend, fences to repair, fallen trees to saw into logs. No one had an eye for the sea but Ellen, daydreaming in the watchtower, skimming the waves in her imaginary schooner, cutting through the shimmering ocean like a gull on the wing. And look! Here was another ship on the horizon, a two-master like her own!

The fire in the grate hissed. Ellen leaped to her feet.

The ship was going much too fast, listing to starboard and heading straight for the rocks at the end of the headland.

All islanders, royal or not, know what to do when a ship is in peril. Ellen dashed across the room to the bell rope, seized it in both hands, and pulled.

And pulled.

And pulled.

When the whole castle was ringing with the clang of the alarm bell, she gathered her skirts to her knees and raced down the stairs yelling, "Ship in peril! Ship in peril, to the east of the headland!" As she burst into the hall, the rescue crew were already running for the main gates, making for Taransay Bay where their mates were pushing the island's three lifeboats into the water.

The boats were built for storm and tempest, with eight strong oarsmen each, but as Ellen slipped in among the crowd, the mood was somber.

Every island family had lost a loved one to the sea.

Was it wrong, wondered Ellen, to feel a little bit excited?

In, out, tumbled the tide, while a handful of men battled wind and waves. The troubled schooner surged in the swell. For a few seconds, they saw her outlined against the gray-streaked sky. Then she crashed from sight.

The islanders bowed their heads. Only Ellen kept watching.

What must it feel like, to conquer such waves?

All the lifeboats had vanished too—no, she glimpsed two of them! But where was the third?

"She's gone!" The woman standing beside Ellen began to wail. "The *Florrie*'s gone, and my Duncan with her!"

But there was the *Florrie* as well, pulling ahead from the *Gordania* and the *Gavenia*, and every last person on the strand cheered at the sight of her.

There was no sight, though, of the schooner.

"She's run into the reef!" A runner came down from Taransay Lighthouse. "The lads are picking up the crew. Who knows how many they'll come home with!"

Come home they did, each and every one of the rescuers, and with them all of the schooner's crew.

Or so they thought.

"Well done, lads." Bhreac the shipbuilder was also captain of the lifeboat crew. Teeth chattering from cold, he walked among them, shaking hands, slapping shoulders. Islanders rushed forward with brandy and blankets. The king, descended from the castle with Queen Grizel and the princesses, announced that today and for the days to come the castle kitchens would be open to all, that the sailors might eat their fill.

It was only when the final count was made that the schooner captain realized his son was missing.

Bhreac's heart sank. The wind was calming, the color of the waves returning to normal, but his lads were exhausted, and surely this was tempting luck too far.

"We can't leave the boy, Bhreac."

It was Duncan, master of the *Florrie*. And he was right, of course.

"I need seven volunteers!" Bhreac shouted.

But nobody was listening, because another cry had gone up.

A pale blue-and-yellow dory was already on the waves, letters of gold glinting on its prow and a small princess at the oars. . . .

ᏟᏜ * ᏟᏜ

Ellen laughed as she rowed. This was mad! It was terrifying!

It was exciting. . . .

The *Princess of the High Seas* rode the waves like a leaf on an angry wind, Ellen's stomach flipping with every pitch and pull, but she never thought of turning back. She knew exactly where the boy would be. The schooner had foundered by Mendel Rocks. Given the incoming tide and the current, he would be washed up on the secret beach at the foot of the Black Cliffs. It was one of Ellen's favorite places. She could row there in her sleep if she had to, but it would disappear with the high tide, and then the boy would be lost. All she had to do was keep her head and keep rowing.

And beat the tide . . .

And hope that he was still alive . . .

A wave broke over the side, catching her full in the face. She dropped her oar and lurched to grab it before it vanished. The *Princess* rocked as she thumped back into her seat. Ellen's lip was cut and her mouth full of blood—but there was the beach and there, as she had known he would be, was the boy, face down in the sand.

A wave hurtled the *Princess* toward the shore. Ellen raised her oars.

"Ahoy there!"

The undertow swept her back out. Ellen lowered the oars, pulled around to face the beach, and raised them again as the next wave carried her in.

"Ahoy there! Ahoy! Ahoy!"

Still the boy did not move, and Ellen could have wept. Dead! Drowned, when she was so close!

"AHOY THERE! GET UP, YOU IDIOT! DON'T BE DEAD! GET UP!"

He stirred, raised himself on all fours, retched in the water. Another wave broke, and he collapsed.

There was almost no beach left.

"GET UP! GET UP, I CAN'T DO THIS ON MY OWN!"

He was on his knees again . . . staggering to his feet . . . limping through the shallows. . . . Ellen threw her rope. He caught it on the next wave, pulled himself to the boat . . .

She heaved him over the side and he tumbled to the floor.

"Ahoy there," he croaked, with a flicker of a smile.

"Ahoy," she grinned back, and her life changed forever.

ᗯ) * ᘓ)

Next day, on a calm sea, the coast guards rowed out again to drag the remains of the schooner back to shore. With a huge hole in her hull, her interiors ruined, her masts broken, and her sails torn to tatters, the *Gallante Héloïse* was ruined but not entirely wrecked.

"It'll take months to make her seaworthy again," Bhreac warned. "And when she is, she'll be more new ship than old."

The *Héloïse*'s sailors found lodgings where they could with the villagers, but the officers, including the captain and his son, were guests at the castle. All through the autumn and the winter, Ellen and the boy—his name was Ralf—carried on the conversation that had started with those first ahoys. While the good weather lasted, she showed him the treasures of her island, the sea caves where the echoes of the waves sounded like music, the cliffs where the gulls nested, and the burrows to which the puffins returned every summer to raise their young. When winter came and the boats were put away, they sat in the watchtower and he told her what it was like to travel the oceans from east to west and back again, to see the color of the sea change from gray to clearest blue. He told her about the desert he had once visited with his father, where marble palaces glowed like fire

in the setting sun, and about forests full of parrots that screeched like a person being murdered and that could be trained to mimic human speech.

"They like the rudest words best," he said, and Ellen snorted with laughter.

Ralf spoke of docks where merchants came from all over the world to trade in silks and spices, of whales and dolphins and turtles and flying fish, and of days on end at sea when all that happened was the rising of the sun and its setting.

Ellen longed for that most of all.

"Take me with you when you leave," she begged, and

Ralf said that he would, and that together they would sail the world.

"It will end badly," said the king, watching them together. "I don't like it."

And still the queen said nothing.

ꞶꙨ * ꙨꞶ

Spring arrived, and the *Gallante Héloïse* was ready. With her black hull and white sails, she was the smartest ship Ellen had ever seen. The day before she was due to sail, the captain invited the royal family aboard, and she ran all over the *Héloïse* like a child, delighting in the smallest details—the shine of the ship's wheel, the coop where the chickens were kept, the neat galley kitchen. She leaned over the prow to admire the restored figurehead of Héloïse herself, she slid down narrow stairs to inspect the hold, she admired the spick-and-span captain's cabin and swung in one of the sailors' hammocks.

"Which is to be mine?" she asked.

No one spoke. Ralf stared at his father. The king stared at his feet. When Grizel gently laid her hand on her daughter's arm, Ellen knew that there was no hammock for her, and never had been.

"Dearest, you are still so very young," said Grizel.

"More to the point," grumbled the king, "you are a *princess*."

"Pa won't take you against your parents' wishes," Ralf explained later, when they were sitting in the *Princess* for the last time, on the beach where Ellen had rescued him. "Not when he's accepted their hospitality for so long. He says it would be a betrayal of trust."

"I could stow away!" said Ellen.

"I thought of that already," Ralf replied gloomily. "But you'd have to come out sooner or later, and then Pa would only bring you back."

Next day, as he boarded the *Héloïse*, he gave her a present, a gold mirror on a piece of scarlet ribbon.

"I pulled it up in a fishing net," he said. "It's proper treasure. Keep it safe for me until I come back."

And with those words, he sailed away.

ᚺᚺ ✷ ᚺᚺ

Spring turned to summer,

summer to autumn, and winter came again. Many ships docked on Rhain, but none were the *Gallante Héloïse*. At first Ellen wore the mirror on her belt, to remind herself that Ralf would be back soon, but with the passing of each season, something in her passed too, and she put the mirror away. She could not bear to look at it, just as she could not bear to watch the sea. When spring returned, she did not race to the shipyard to reclaim her overwintered boat, but sat meekly with her sisters and asked to learn to sew.

Grizel helped her thread a needle.

"Sailors need to sew too, you know," she murmured. "Sailcloth does not mend itself."

"I shall never sail again," said Ellen.

Along came summer, and as Ellen sat quietly sewing, a screech fit to freeze blood ripped through the castle, followed by a stream of filthy language.

"Goodness!" gasped Catriona.

"Who can it be?" tutted Ailsa.

Iseabail fanned herself with her stitching and looked as if she might faint.

Ellen's heart skipped a beat. Somewhere in the string of unrepeatable language, she thought she had heard her name. . . .

There was another screech, and more swearing, and then—

"I come for the Princess Ellen!"

Hope smote her like a blow to the chest. Dropping her needlework, she leaped from her chair as a red-faced footman entered.

"If you please," he stammered. "There appears to be a parrot . . . "

ᙅᔑ * ᙅᔑ

The parrot was the first of many gifts Ralf sent Ellen over the years. It was followed by a box of spices, each carefully labeled, and then by books of maritime history, maps, more maps, and a compass. Ellen, the mirror once more hanging at her belt, read every word and memorized every chart. She brought the *Princess of the High Seas* out of hibernation and sailed farther, better, and faster than she had ever sailed before. And when, six years after he had left, Ralf returned at the helm of his own command, she was ready, and pressed the mirror into his hand, and took her place at his side.

"Preposterous!" railed the king. "A princess of Rhain!"

Still Queen Grizel said nothing, though it grieved her to lose her favorite child. She had always known that if you give a dreamer hope, her dreams will get bigger and bigger, and that if you give an adventurous child a boat, sooner or later she will sail away.

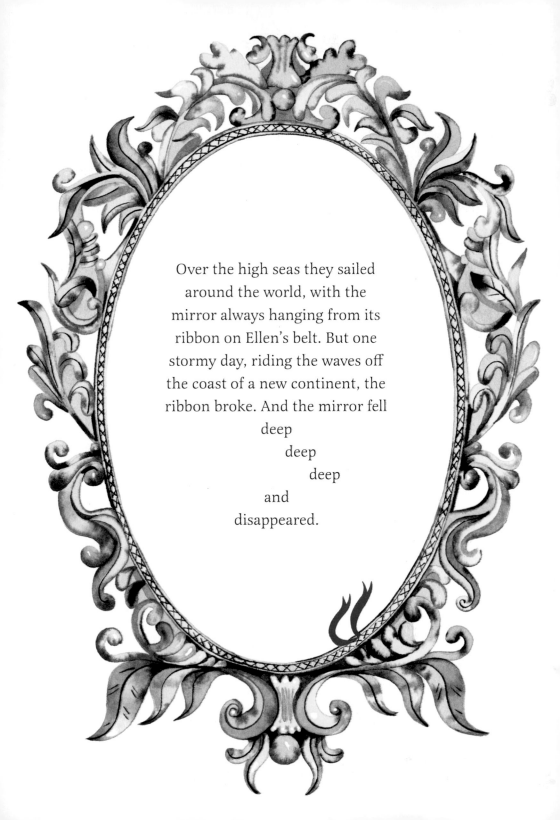

Over the high seas they sailed
around the world, with the
mirror always hanging from its
ribbon on Ellen's belt. But one
stormy day, riding the waves off
the coast of a new continent, the
ribbon broke. And the mirror fell
deep
    deep
        deep
and
disappeared.

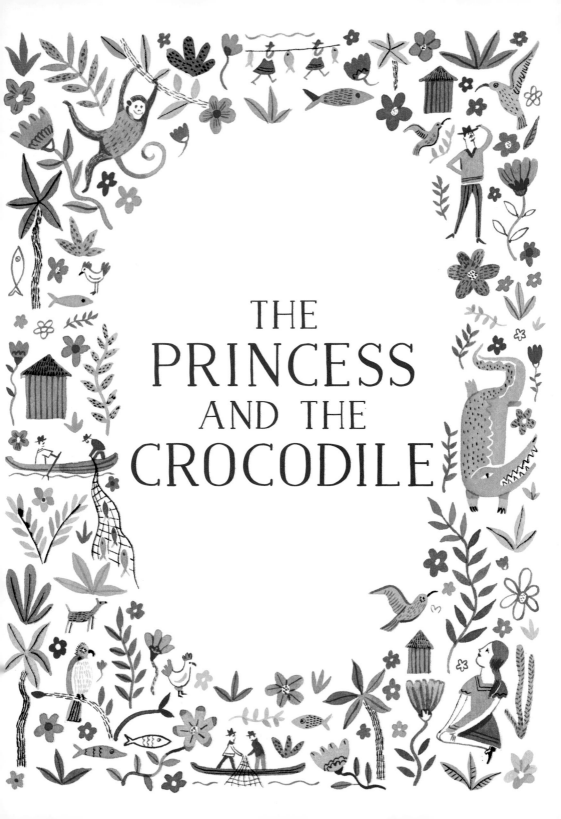

THE
PRINCESS
AND THE
CROCODILE

THE
PRINCESS
AND THE
CROCODILE

T he fishermen rescued the little crocodile
because it was stuck alone on a log in the
middle of a forest backwater and appeared
to be choking. Under normal circumstances,
they would have ignored him and left him to die or
survive on his own. They were tough men, used to
killing things. They were not sentimental about the
cocodrilos, who could snatch a child from the shore
and drag it under in a blossom of blood, faster than a
heartbeat. But these were not normal circumstances.
Today they were fishing with Old José, who was
sentimental about everything.

"Poor thing," Old José said, before asking did they
know that when his grandmother's grandmother

had been a girl, crocodiles had been sacred on the peninsula, and worshipped as gods?

Pepe sighed and said that, yes, he had heard the stories many times.

"We should take him to the chief's daughter," Old José decided. "She'll know what to do with him."

Fernando, who was even less interested than Pepe in stories or gods or even grandmothers, asked what the chief's daughter was going to do with a flaming great crocodile.

"It's not a flaming great crocodile, it's a baby," said Old José. "Look how dainty he is, no longer than my

arm. And the *princesita* is good with animals. Think of the hummingbirds."

They smiled as they thought of seven-year-old Tica and the hummingbirds she had raised from chicks. Everywhere she went, the birds flew around her head like a multicolored crown.

Still. "A *cocodrilo* isn't a hummingbird," pointed out Pepe. "And babies grow. I say the only good crocodile is a dead one and we kill it right now."

The baby crocodile hiccupped.

"Bless him," said Old José.

And that was that, because, maddening though he

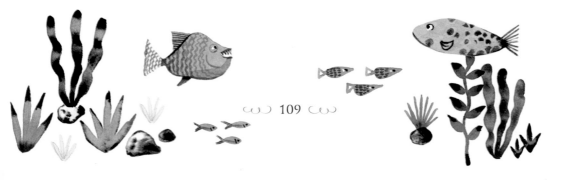

was, nobody wanted to upset the old man. Fernando swore but picked up the startled crocodile, Pepe tied a rope around his snout to stop him snapping, and together they bundled him into their boat and carried him to the chief's daughter.

They found Tica sitting in her parents' garden in the shade of a passion-fruit tree, wreathed in hummingbirds and playing with an orphaned spider monkey.

"Brought you another rescue, princess," said Old José.

Fernando, with a nothing-to-do-with-me kind of grunt, deposited the crocodile in her lap.

The birds swirled to the branches above, and the monkey swiftly followed, but Tica gave a cry of delight.

"A crocodile! *Señor* José! I have always dreamed of making friends with a crocodile. . . . Oh, he's soft as a kitten! But what's wrong with him? It sounds like he can't breathe."

She pulled a knife from the pocket of her dress. The fishermen held their breath as she sliced through the ropes binding the baby reptile's snout. Fernando winced and looked away as she pried apart his jaws.

"Hold his mouth open," she ordered José. Oblivious to the rows of sharp, pointy teeth, she peered down the crocodile's throat, then plunged her arm into his gullet. Old José held firm as the creature gagged and strained to snap his jaws.

Tica fished carefully inside the crocodile's throat until her fingers closed around something flat and hard and she began, very gently, to pull it out. Everybody crowded around to stare. The object Tica held was made of gold. Once she had wiped off the crocodile spit and slime, they saw that it was ornately engraved, with a scrap of tattered red ribbon tied through a loop at one end, and a clasp at the other.

"What is it?" asked Pepe.

Cautiously, Tica pressed the clasp. The object opened up like a seashell.

"It's a mirror!"

"Seems small for a mirror," said Fernando. "What's the use of that? And how'd it get inside a crocodile?"

"Someone must have dropped it in the water." Tica frowned at her reflection. She did not approve of people dropping things in the water, precisely because so often they ended up being eaten by animals. Still, it wasn't the mirror's fault. She rubbed it on her skirt. It was pretty. Polished, and with

a fresh ribbon, it would be even prettier. She slid it into her pocket next to her knife.

"I'll keep it," she said. "And I'll keep the crocodile too." She dropped a kiss on the creature's nose. "You'd like that, wouldn't you? To live here with us, and be my friend?"

The crocodile dropped its snout in her lap and blinked adoring yellow eyes.

"The gods will thank us," said Old José. "You'll see."

The fishermen still weren't convinced.

"I wouldn't have rescued it if I'd known she was going to keep it," grumbled Fernando as they returned to their nets. "It's one thing stopping an animal suffering, but having it live with us!"

"What about our children?" asked his wife, Maia, washing clothes in the river while her young son kept watch for other, larger crocodiles. "He'll attack them, for sure."

"He'll eat our cows and pigs too!" said Lilia, Pepe's wife.

"We must tell the chief we don't want the creature," the villagers decided. "He's a sensible man. He must order Tica to let the crocodile go."

So they went to the chief, and he wholeheartedly agreed. He *was* a sensible man, and he had no desire to live with a crocodile, however soft and pretty.

"Crocodiles belong in the river," he informed his daughter. "They are not like hummingbirds. They cannot be tamed."

"And think of what crocodiles do!" Tica's mother cried. "The danger to the children! The pigs and cattle!"

But Tica was stubborn, and perhaps a tiny bit spoiled. She was used to getting her way.

"If you don't let me keep him," she replied, "I will swim away with him, and though I know that *he* would never eat me, another crocodile probably would, and *then* you'll be sorry."

She glared at them. So did the crocodile. And who knows where the conversation would have ended, with angry villagers on one side and a fierce child on the other, and a chief torn between the two, if the cry hadn't gone up from the river at that very moment?

"My baby, oh, my baby!"

Everyone ran to the jetty, to see Pepe and Lilia's two-year-old daughter, Jacinta, swept away by the current, around the river bend, vanishing from sight.

The fishermen put out in their boats at once, but without hope. No matter how fast they paddled, or how well they rode the current, they were no match for the river, and a small child even less so. Jacinta would drown, and her body would be eaten by wild animals.

It was what happened when you lived by the water. If it wasn't the current, it was snakes or crocodiles, and there was nothing to be done about it. The children wailed in this terrible knowledge. Their parents pulled them closer. Lilia rocked backward and forward on the sand. And then . . .

"They've found her!"

Lilia began to sob, then laugh, as a canoe reappeared, rowing upstream in the quiet channel on the far side of the river, Pepe seated at the back with his daughter in his arms, dripping and sniffing but also waving and shouting, "Mama! Mama!"

The villagers cheered—then, one by one, fell silent.

"Well, will you look at that?" whispered Maia.

The little crocodile stood on the end of the jetty, his slim young body quivering as he stretched his snout low over the water, for all the world as if he were singing to it.

"The gods have blessed us," murmured Old José.

And the little crocodile stayed.

Tica named him Choro, after the people who once worshipped crocodiles as gods, and from the very first day they were devoted to each other. Choro went everywhere with Tica, and it was wonderful how quickly the villagers grew used to the sight of him scurrying after her on his stubby legs on land, and to the sound of her singing to him as he swam beside her when she explored the river and its backwaters

in her canoe. He slept in her bedroom, and he was as much a part of the chief's daughter as her crown of hummingbirds and the monkey on her shoulder. The villagers grew bolder with him themselves. Children threw balls in the river for him to fetch, and visitors to the chief's house grew used to stepping over him as he sunned himself on the warm stone doorstep. And when sometimes they saw him with his snout stretched low over the river as he had done on the day Jacinta was saved, they were careful to speak in whispers and to walk on tiptoe so as not to disturb him.

A year to the day after Old José had rescued Choro, and Choro had sung to the river to rescue Jacinta, a grandmother who, like José, knew of the old ways, brought her baby granddaughter to the crocodile for blessing. She walked up to where he lay basking and placed Teresita, dressed all in white lace, before him. The villagers held their breath as Choro opened his yellow eyes and gently breathed a crocodile kiss over her.

From then on, every baby born in the village was brought before him.

They called Choro *el milagro*—the miracle—because once he came to the village, there was not another crocodile attack or even a crocodile sighting, and not one child drowned.

The villagers were blessed, and they rejoiced.

In time, though, they forgot that blessings work both ways and that neglected gods become vengeful.

∽ * ∽

Babies grow, human and crocodile. When the fishermen first brought Choro to Tica, when he was

two and she was seven, they could lie side by side with the tip of his tail level with her feet, and the end of his snout at her shoulder. But by the time Tica was twelve, Choro was twice her size. The limbs that had seemed so dainty to Old José were thick, his kitten-soft scales were rough and gnarled, his light, graceful body was heavy. He grew too long to sleep alongside Tica's bed, too wide for people to step over on the sunny doorstep.

"Drat that blundering lizard!" exclaimed Lilia, as she tripped over his tail.

"Lumbering nuisance!" grumbled Teresita's father, when Choro upset his woodpile.

"Ugly brute, isn't he?" commented visitors who had previously wished for a holy crocodile of their own.

Choro still followed Tica where he could, but a twelve-year-old girl is not as free as a seven-year-old, especially when she is a chief's daughter. Tica had to spend more time with her mother now, learning how to cook and sew, how to tend a garden and to mix plants for medicine. She never had time to scratch Choro's head just where he liked it, or lie against his flank to sunbathe, or go out with him swimming by her canoe. Now, every day, he swam alone. Without Tica's

songs to keep him at the surface, he dived deeper and deeper. Weightless and powerful, down where fish darted and eels snaked through the green, swaying weeds, he forgot the human world. Sometimes he felt the flow of the river shift and he sensed his own kind were near. Every day he searched for them, farther and farther, until one morning he reached the place where the river roared into the sea. Here, where the world was flooded with light, where soft water turned to salt and mud turned to sand on a hot bright triangle of land, he came across a dozen creatures just like him and he knew that he was home.

And yet he still loved Tica. And so, as day fell and the sand cooled, he slid away from that place to swim back to her. But something in him had changed. On

the edge of the village, when a shadow fell over the water, he surged toward it. The shadow put up a fight, but it was no match for the crocodile. It was gone faster than a heartbeat. In a blossom of blood.

The gods need looking after if you want to keep them on your side.

Choro dragged the calf to a backwater island, because he was hungry and that is what crocodiles do. After he had eaten, he slept, half-hidden in the reeds, through what was left of the day and through the night and again through most of the following day. When he woke, guided by habit and still by love, he swam home, and because he was a pet as well as a wild animal, he did not look out for danger where he had always been safe.

He didn't notice the nets the villagers had set to catch him, or the men lining the bank with spears to kill him, or the poles they had readied to carry him back from the water, or the fire on which they planned to burn him as an offering to some new god. And when he did swim into their trap, he didn't understand and, just as when they found him as a baby, fought and struggled to breathe.

"Now we've got him!" the fishermen cried. "Now we've got the devil!"

Deep in Choro's reptile heart he knew that something sweet was missing, something like birdsong or the warmth of the sun. But he was drowning now, and he could not remember. Shadows were coming closer, many shadows brandishing sticks, and he knew that they were coming for him and that he was going to die.

Choro's great body shook with his final sigh. Two round tears fell from his yellow eyes as he closed them and then he was going, he was gone except . . .

"If you don't release him *this minute*," said a clear strong voice, "I will swim far away in the river and another crocodile will probably eat me and *then* you'll be sorry."

The voice was not as soft as once it was, but he knew it, and though he did not understand the words, he understood their meaning.

He opened his eyes. Tica stood beside him in the water, and in her hand she held the same knife she had once used to unmuzzle him all those years ago when they were both much smaller. When she had cut through the last of the nets that strangled him, she dropped a kiss on his snout as she had done on that very first day, and then she was crying, and pushing him away, and he sank deep, deep, deep into the dark green water, and left her.

The villagers went back to fearing crocodiles, and the crocodiles went back to attacking them, because that is the way, on the river.

But for many years they told stories of a time long ago, when one of the great beasts lived among them and was their friend. And some day, if you are very lucky, you might see an old woman paddling her canoe, and beside her in the water will be a giant crocodile, and she will be singing to him.

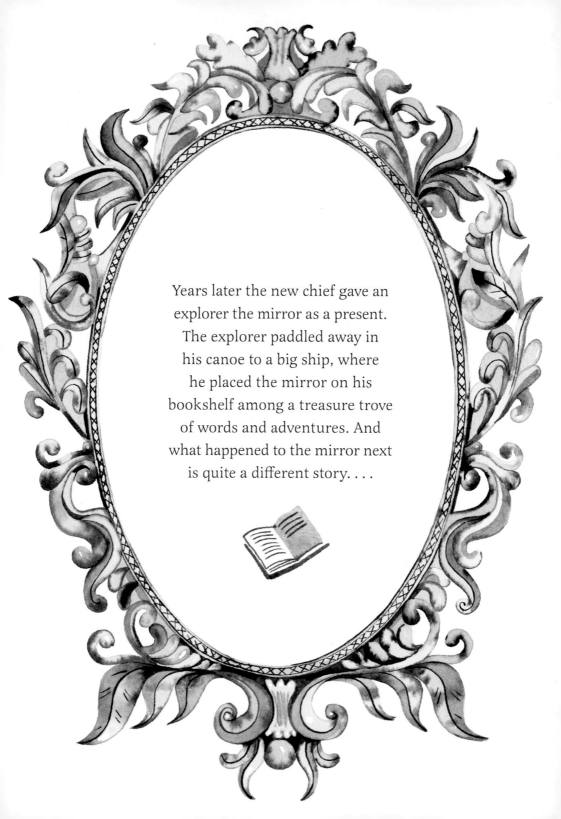

Years later the new chief gave an
explorer the mirror as a present.
The explorer paddled away in
his canoe to a big ship, where
he placed the mirror on his
bookshelf among a treasure trove
of words and adventures. And
what happened to the mirror next
is quite a different story. . . .

THE
STORY
PRINCESS

THE STORY PRINCESS

Once upon a time, on a misty, rain-swept island, there was a castle.

It was splendid, with turrets and towers, moats and battlements, gardens and ballrooms, and the princes and princesses who lived there were equally splendid. Each had a particular talent. Prince Ruaríg was a champion swimmer who had once rescued the king's favorite dog from drowning; Princess Fionnula's singing made her famous all over the country; Princess Aoife was a fearless horse rider; Prince Pádraig's dancing was exquisite; and, at the age of ten, Prince Connor could shoot an arrow straight and true.

Only Princess Saoirse was different.

Saoirse sang like a frog, danced like a goat, had never learned to swim, and was afraid of animals. The one time she had tried to shoot an arrow, everyone had laughed because she almost killed the cat, and she had sulked for days.

"Why am I so strange?" she asked her mother one day.

"You're not strange, darling!" the queen protested. "You're *different*."

"I *am* strange," Saoirse retorted. "Everybody says so. Yesterday, one of your ladies called me an 'odd little thing,' and another one said, 'yes, what a shame, when the others are so marvelous.' I *heard* them. I was hiding in the hedge when they were walking in the garden. I hate it when they compare me to the others!"

"You shouldn't eavesdrop," said the queen. "And what were you hiding from?"

"*Everything*," said Saoirse.

The queen's heart bled for her daughter. *Hiding in hedges!* she wrote to her own mother. *She is a bit odd . . . but, Mama, I think she is also lonely. Please will you come to visit, and try to talk to her? You are so wise, I am sure you will know exactly what to say.*

The old queen was indeed wise. So wise, in fact,

that when she came she did not try to talk to her
granddaughter at all. Instead, she gave her a book.

"Why?" asked Saoirse.

"If you prefer," her grandmother replied, "we can
watch Connor practice his archery."

Saoirse opened the book.

THE PRINCESS IN THE MIRROR

As the hare runs fleet and the hawk flies true
I will find my way to you
Before the strike of twelve
Before the closing of the gate
I will bring you home

Rose came into this world on a crisp spring morning, as farmhands drove cattle back to the fields from milking and the school bell in the village started to ring. After the birth, the midwife turned her back on mother and baby for less than a minute and went to the window. The ground lurched as she pushed it open, and for a moment the world was thick with mist. The midwife wondered confusedly if there might be an earthquake. But when she looked out of the window she saw only order and loveliness. A robin sang from a branch of the old oak tree in the garden, a ring of tiny white cyclamen grew at its foot. From the lane, she heard children laughing on their way to school, and she smiled at the thought that, one day, the new baby would walk that same path.

All this the midwife noticed, yet it did not strike

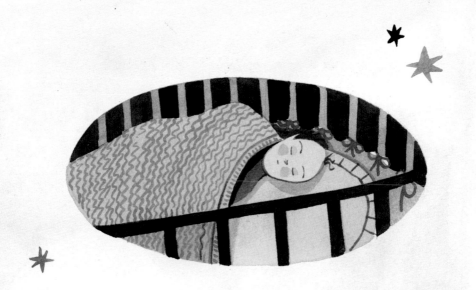

her as strange that, though the day was still, the leaves of the oak tree shook as if a storm was blowing. She did not hear the scurrying footsteps, the thud as something small and round slipped through a gap in the floorboards. And when she turned back to the white-green baby in the cot, she forgot that the baby she had laid there only moments before had been plump and pink.

Even the mother forgot.

It was as if a spell had been cast.

Francis and Eileen, the parents, loved the child with all their hearts. They were honest farmers who went to the local market every week and to the town fair twice a year. Otherwise they lived quietly in their old farmhouse on the edge of the village. Which was just as well, because after Rose arrived, their neighbors kept away.

"Strange..." whispered the ironmonger's wife, when she saw the white-green baby.

"Creepy," said the baker. "I'll not be letting *my* children near her."

"In the old days," said the mayor's housekeeper, "they would say she was not of this world. They would have left her in the forest to fend for herself..."

A child left in the forest meant a child eaten by wolves. Everyone knew that.

No one said, "Thank goodness those days are over."

The years passed and the neighbors' disapproval grew.

"Her clothes!" they whispered, whenever Rose passed. "Dear me, her clothes!"

It wasn't that Rose's clothes were *different*. Eileen dressed her in exactly the same plain, hard-wearing dresses as all the village girls. Yet as soon as Rose put

them on, the itchy pinafores and stiff aprons that hung so heavy on others became airy as silk, swirling and billowing like something alive. Her parents thought this was beautiful, but the neighbors knew it wasn't right, just as Rose's silver eyes weren't right, or her wild black hair that no ribbon could hold. As for the way she behaved! Who could forget Rose's first morning at school, when instead of playing with the other children, she had climbed right to the top of the rowan tree by the gate? She had stayed there all day. When asked why, she said she was keeping company with a robin.

A robin! And how had a child so small even gotten *into* the tree, let alone to the top?

There were always so many questions about Rose, and always so few answers. . . .

Her classmates made up a song about her, and no wonder, the neighbors muttered. It wasn't a nice song—but then, they muttered, Rose wasn't a nice child.

A few days before Rose's twelfth birthday, their disapproval reached new heights. A crowd had gathered to gossip in the square, where Rose in rippling tweed lay on the wall of the mayor's paddock, ignoring them and singing to his horse with her hair full of straw.

"I heard she is sleeping *outside*," the mayor's housekeeper whispered. "In a *haystack*! Like a *rat*!"

"But whatever *for*?" cried the ironmonger's wife.

"She has"—the mayor's housekeeper lowered her voice even further—"*dreams*!"

"Dreams?"

"Bad dreams, Eileen says, if she sleeps in a bed. *Scary* dreams. I ask you! Eileen should send the girl away."

"Oh, yes," said the ironmonger's wife and the baker and several others, smug because *their* daughters did not flaunt their clothes, or sing to animals, or sleep in haystacks, or dream. "Eileen should send her away."

No one mentioned the wolves, but they were all thinking of them.

"As the hare runs fleet and the hawk flies true
I will find my way to you."

Rose pulled the horse's ears as she sang. She liked
horses. They were not as quick as birds or as clever as
foxes, but their solid strength was soothing, and after
last night she needed to be soothed.

For as long as she could remember, there had been
only one dream. A forest, cool and dark, though bright
with flowers where the light broke through. Loud with
birdsong, alive with animals and—people.

People who looked like her.

They slept in trees, the people in her dreams. Foraged for nuts and berries, drank from streams, hunted with knives and arrows. They were tough and fierce, always running and climbing. Rose thought they must be at war, because though she never saw them fight, she often dreamed of them returning, bloody and battered, to the forest. But, oh, the wild freedom when at night, around their fires, they set aside their troubles and began to dance and sing! And the ease with which they moved among the treetops— leaping from branch to branch as if they were flying! Just thinking about it took Rose's breath away.

Sometimes, waking up was more than she could bear.

Rose had not been entirely truthful with Eileen about why she wanted to sleep outside. It wasn't that her dreams were scary. It was more that they were so *big* she felt they might tear down the walls.

"Sometimes," she whispered to the horse, "when I'm inside, I can't breathe."

The horse tossed its head.

"Poor dear," she said. "You probably feel like that every time they put the bit in your mouth."

The horse sighed. Rose dropped a kiss on its nose. A group of girls passing began to chant.

"Changeling, witch, goblin child
Dirty, stupid, ugly, wild."

It was the song they had made up about her at school on the first day, the song that followed her everywhere. Rose bit her lip and ignored them.

In yesterday's dream, dancers had spun through flames to the sound of drums, while singers held hands in a circle around the blazing fires, singing of love and life and death. When Rose awoke, her pillow was wet with tears.

"There's a girl in my dreams," she whispered to the horse. "She's different from them, like I'm different here, all pink and white, with soft straight hair. She tries to keep up with them, but she slows them down, and I don't think they like it. There's a woman who cares for her who always seems sad. They're looking for something, these two, all the time—they search every tree trunk, every stone, every inch of forest floor. Usually the others ignore them, but last night . . . "

Last night, some of the forest people had threatened the girl and the woman. Rose didn't know what they had said. She only knew that even though the girl had cried and the woman had pleaded, the forest people had turned their backs on them. Afterward, the woman had held the girl and sang to her, the song that Rose was singing now.

The song she *always* sang.

"As the hare runs fleet and the hawk flies true . . . "

A gaggle of boys approached, waving sticks. Rose braced herself for their sneers, then frowned as they passed without comment. Something was wrong— the boys always laughed at her. She sat up, craning to listen—heard shouts, laughter, and something else . . .

Rose swung her legs over the wall, floated to the ground, and ran across the square to the front of the crowd. A dog cowered in the middle of the tight circle, a one-eared stray bitch Rose knew well, the mother of six eight-week-old puppies. Her jaw was locked onto

a shoulder of lamb stolen from a kitchen, and she was growling as the boys jabbed her with their sticks.

"Let it go, thief!"

The bitch whimpered as a blow caught her on the side of the head, but she did not let go.

Rose cried out. The bitch, sensing an ally, dashed toward her and cowered against her legs. Rose reached down to pat her.

"Get out of the way, freak," growled Thom, the oldest boy.

"I won't!"

"I'll beat you if you don't!"

"Go on, then!"

> *"Changeling, witch, goblin child*
> *Dirty, stupid, ugly, wild."*

It happened very fast. One moment, the boys were circling Rose, jeering. The next, they were spinning out of control, faster and faster, until their feet were off the ground—as if they were flying, people said. Then, suddenly, they stopped and fell. Thom broke his collarbone, another boy broke his wrist, two others suffered concussions, and everyone said Rose had done it.

The next day, Francis and Eileen received a visit from the mayor.

"But how could Rose have done it?" cried Eileen.

"One small girl against four strong lads!" agreed her husband. "It's not possible!"

And yet, the mayor said, the lads were injured and the girl was not.

"There is a place in town," he added.

"What sort of place?" asked Eileen.

"A school."

"But Rose goes to school here!"

"A good place for girls like her," the mayor plowed on. "Where they'll teach Rose right from wrong and drive wild thoughts from her head. She'll come back a changed girl."

Eileen thought of the only time she had taken Rose to town, how she had hated it—the clatter of metal cart wheels on stone streets, blinkered horses, and every tree or patch of grass hemmed by walls or railings.

"But we don't want her changed," she whispered. "We love her as she is."

"They are calling her a witch," said the mayor.

"Dirty, ugly, stupid, wild . . . "

In her head, Eileen heard the howl of wolves. She knew what people did to witches.

Rose watched them come for her from the window of her parents' bedroom, on the morning of her birthday, as farmhands drove cattle back to the fields from milking and the school bell rang. The mayor and the women from the town school came in a cart; villagers followed on foot. The women from town wore black and looked like crows.

Her parents were waiting by the gate. Francis had his arm around Eileen. Rose felt her eyes prickle.

The cart stopped. The mayor glanced up as he climbed down. Rose dropped out of sight and curled into a ball on the floor behind the curtain.

"Rose!" Francis, trying to sound brave. "Rose, love, it's time!"

Rose ran her fingers along a gap in the floorboards and wished that she could hide there.

"Rose, come down!"

There was something lodged between the boards, something shiny. The gap was wide enough for her little finger. She hooked it through a scrap of ribbon and tugged.

The something shiny was a mirror compact, gold and etched with flowers, quite out of place in the farmhouse. What was it doing there? Rose ran her fingers over it, then pressed the clasp on its side. . . .

The ground lurched and she dropped the mirror. The window blew open and the world disappeared in a thick white mist. Rose scrambled to her feet and fought back a scream.

The pink-and-white girl from her dreams was standing before her.

For a few seconds, all either girl could do was stare. Then the girl from Rose's dreams rushed forward to grasp her hands.

"It's you! Oh, it is you! But how did you do it?"

Rose swallowed. "Do what?"

"How did you open the portal?"

"I . . . looked in a mirror?"

"A mirror! Clever Aisling! Oh, I'm so happy to see you!"

Despite her astonishment, Rose felt a glow of pleasure. She couldn't remember anyone apart from her parents *ever* being happy to see her. Except . . .

"My name's not Aisling."

"Why, what do they call you here? Rose? That's a terrible name for you! Though perfect for me! Oh, now you look confused. I'll explain, but quickly! We—you and I—we were born at the same time, exactly twelve years ago. Me here, you in the forest realm. But there was a war in the forest, so the midwife who delivered you hid you here, to keep you safe, because you're a princess . . . "

"A *princess*?"

" . . . and they wanted to kidnap you. Oh, there's no *time* for this! The midwife who hid you was killed before she could explain how her portal worked, but the point is portals only last twelve years and today . . . "

"Today is our birthday," Rose said slowly. *"Before the strike of twelve . . . "*

"*Before the closing of the gate* . . . You know the song! Your mother sings it all the time."

"The woman in my dream is my *mother*?"

"She's never stopped searching for you. Aisling, you will go back, won't you? The forest people, they're good people, but I slow them down and after the portal closes, some of them want to leave me in the forest, and there are *wolves* . . ."

Something was happening. The white mist was thinning, the room coming back into focus. Outside the door, Aisling (she *was* Aisling, she knew it) heard footsteps.

"There are wolves here too," she said. "Human wolves, and human crows. Are you afraid?"

"No!" said Rose (she was Rose, just as Aisling was Aisling). "Are you afraid of the war?"

"I don't think so," said Aisling.

"Love, it's time!" Eileen was on the landing. For a wild moment, all Aisling wanted was to run into her arms. But then, outside, the village children took up their chant. . . .

"Changeling, witch, goblin
child . . . "

"Aisling!" Rose was fading with the mist. "The mirror! We're running out of time. The mirror is the portal. Pick it up and bring it here—let's hold it together. . . . "

The girls clasped their fingers around the mirror and held their breath.

Nothing happened.

"Close your eyes!" urged Rose. "Wish!"

The chanting grew louder, the door handle turned, and suddenly . . .

Aisling knew what she must do.

She let go of Rose's hand, let go of the mirror. As the door opened, she jumped onto the sill. As Eileen, Francis, and the mayor entered the room, she spread her arms . . .

. . . and flew.

The mirror glowed. The ground lurched, the world filled with mist. Eileen, bursting into the room, wondered about earthquakes, but when the mist cleared and the ground leveled, she saw only order and loveliness. A robin sang in the old oak tree, and a ring of tiny white cyclamen grew at its foot, while outside in the lane children laughed on their way to school.

"Happy birthday, love!" Eileen hugged her pink-and-white daughter close. "Twelve years old already! Where does the time go? Now hurry or you'll be late for school!"

The mayor returned to the village, the crows went back to town. The children forgot their wicked song about the white-green girl.

Everyone forgot. Well, almost everyone.

The real Rose kept the mirror always, all through her long and happy life. She liked to peep at it from time to time, to see how Aisling was getting on.

Whenever she did, Aisling was always running or climbing or dancing.

It was dark by the time Saoirse finished reading. She closed the book, placed it on the table beside her, and stared thoughtfully at the fire.

"Well?" asked her grandmother. "What did you think?"

"I didn't like the way people treated them," said Saoirse. "They were mean. It wasn't Aisling or Rose's fault they were different."

"The world is not kind to those it does not understand," agreed her grandmother. "But they found a place where someone understood them, didn't they?"

"I know what you're doing," grumbled Saoirse. "Any minute now you're going to say *I'm* not strange, I'm *different*. But the point is, I am *not* a changeling. I can't go and live in the forest. There is nowhere for me to go but this castle."

"But there is." Her grandmother tapped the book on the table between them. "Don't you see? You have been there already."

It was only much later, as she reached for the book again in bed, that the old queen's meaning became clear to Saoirse. She was looking forward to reading the next story, as she imagined looking forward to seeing a friend. And the book *was* a friend, she decided.

Hadn't she run through the forest with Aisling who was Rose, and climbed trees and sung to horses with Rose who was Aisling? Their hearts had beaten in time, her lips had silently mouthed their songs. She had never felt so completely understood as when she was reading their story.

"Maybe," she whispered to herself, "that is what stories do." And then, louder, "The princess who reads stories. That is what I will be. No, not just the princess who reads. The princess who collects stories, and listens to stories, and *tells* stories. I will be the Story Princess."

Saoirse opened the book and began to read. She never even noticed when something small and shiny slipped from between the pages and fell with a quiet thud through a gap in the floorboards. . . .

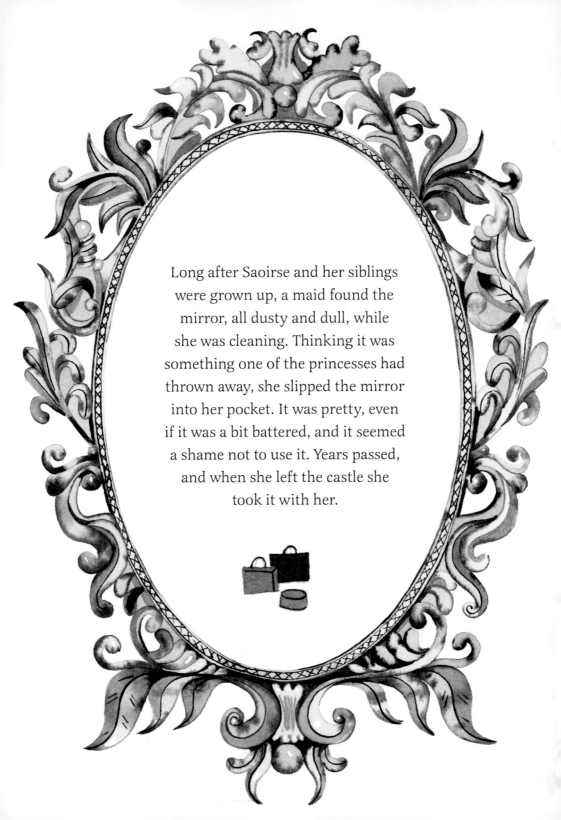

Long after Saoirse and her siblings were grown up, a maid found the mirror, all dusty and dull, while she was cleaning. Thinking it was something one of the princesses had thrown away, she slipped the mirror into her pocket. It was pretty, even if it was a bit battered, and it seemed a shame not to use it. Years passed, and when she left the castle she took it with her.

THE
PRINCESSES
IN EXILE

THE
PRINCESSES
IN EXILE

There were sleighs and horses and a sliver of moon shining on the snow, and it was like scores of other nights, Princesses Sonya, Anya, Petra, and Tatiana cuddled together under blankets. Except tonight there were no bells or laughter, no silk dresses or satin slippers or hot chocolate in silver flasks to drink with spicy cakes. Tonight, no one spoke a word. The princesses wore boots and thick coats and carried water in stone bottles with black bread wrapped in handkerchiefs.

Somewhere in the shadows there were soldiers.

The sisters were running away from war, to a place called the City of Lights, there to find an old duchess cousin they had never met. Deep in the secret pocket of her dress, Sonya carried a gold pocket mirror.

"The duchess and I found it together years ago, frozen in a snowdrift," Mama had told the girls. "She is kind and good. Show it to her and she will help you."

The duchess lived in a grand house on a chic boulevard. There would be dancing again, and parties, and such food! Pastries that melted in the mouth, Mama said, sauces angels must surely eat in heaven, and the bread! Crusty, with a soft white crumb like clouds.

"But I want to stay with you," six-year-old Tatiana had whimpered, while ten-year-old Petra and twelve-year-old Anya and fifteen-year-old Sonya tried to look brave. "I'm not afraid of soldiers. When Petra reads to me, people

never run away. Not if they're the *heroes*."

Mama, who had somehow gathered all four of her daughters in her arms, kissed Tatiana's curls. "Darling Tati, Papa and I will join you by the end of summer for your birthday, I promise."

Petra, who was getting another cold, wheezed, "I suppose it will be an adventure."

"Exactly! Well done, Petra, dear. A splendid adventure, just like a book!"

Splendid! Anya reminded herself now.

SPLENDID.

In the city left behind there had been a palace with rooms painted white and gold and a garden perfect for snowball fights that Anya always won. There had been tea and cream-filled honey cake, stitching with Mama while Papa told stories.

But that was in another life.

Now there was only this sleigh speeding toward a lonely country station, and Tatiana must not wriggle, and Petra must not sneeze, and Sonya must not cry over the beloved grand piano that for obvious reasons could not come too, and Anya must not scream with

rage. They must be quiet as mice because if they were caught, they would be ARRESTED or thrown into the snow and left to FREEZE TO DEATH and this was all part of their *splendid* adventure.

The sleigh stopped long enough for them to clamber out, then took off again into the night.

The princesses were alone.

ᴄᴜᴊ * ᴄᴜᴊ

Through the night and the next day, and another night and another day, the train steamed and puffed. Through forests and snow-covered plains, over rivers and under mountains, past bare winter fields, until the countryside gave way to houses and at last, dirty, exhausted, and starving, they stumbled off the train and into the City of Lights.

There was barely enough money for a cab. Anya stuck her head out of the window as they rattled through the crowded streets. *Why* was it called the City of Lights? Everything was gray—the buildings, the roads, even the people. She thought of home, of sparkling snow, blue skies, the bright colors of the onion domes.

She tried not to think about the soldiers.

The cab rounded a corner into a noisy square, with a dry fountain in the middle and leafless trees all around. Suddenly, a flash caught Anya's eye. She craned to look, glimpsed the name of the square, a haze of pink and blue flowers and something else, a scent, floating over the stink of the street. Anya closed her eyes, and magic happened.

She was in the white-and-gold drawing room at home, with Papa reading and Mama sewing and tea laid out on the table. . . .

They turned another corner and rumbled on. The scent faded, and so did Papa and Mama.

At last the cab turned into a wide, dusty avenue and stopped before a set of carriage gates. The princesses climbed out and stood on the pavement. The gates were rusty, the paint on the side door was flaking, and the bell rope was frayed.

"*Splendid!*" said Petra.

∞ * ∞

In another life, the duchess's house had sparkled. Servants had polished wood and glass and silver, cooks bustled in the kitchen, gardeners tended honeysuckle and roses, guests danced in the ballroom. But war had come, a war that was over—unlike the one back home—but that had left its mark. Now all of the duchess's silver and most of her furniture were

sold, dust lay thick, weeds choked the garden. The only food cooked in the kitchen was soup—endless soup!—made from boiled onions and cabbage stalks and potatoes, and the only guests were refugees. Some moved on after a few weeks. Others, like old Prince Vasily, who walked with two sticks, or the Countess Kaplinska, who was always crying, or Baroness Maranova, who never got out of bed, stayed.

And stayed.

And *stayed*.

None of them had any money. None of them were any *use* to the duchess in the constant battle against the leaking roof, the rising damp, the crumbling brickwork, and the *hunger*.

In another life, the duchess had laughed and danced until her feet hurt, but now, like her house, she was tired.

And then came the princesses.

"Mama told us to show you this." Sonya's hand shook as she held out the mirror.

"She told us all about the snowdrift," coughed Petra.

"She's coming for my birthday," Tatiana yawned.

One child sick, and another practically a baby, the duchess noted—more trouble than they were worth. She fingered the mirror. She had a vague memory of skating on a frozen river, an excited child—the girls' mother?

"She *said* you'd help," scowled Anya.

The duchess looked her up and down. *She might be useful*, she thought. *Her and the older one.*

"You'd have to work," she said. "I can't keep you here for nothing."

"Oh, we're good at working!" said Sonya. "Mama's been teaching us embroidery!"

Embroidery! Four more mouths to feed, and *embroidery*!

"On second thought," said the duchess, "my house is full."

She tried to close the door, but Anya had already pushed past her into the courtyard.

⦅⦆ ∗ ⦅⦆

Three months later, Anya paced the princesses' bedroom like a bear in a cage.

"Sixteen!" she thundered. "That's how many fireplaces the old witch made me scrub today! Sixteen, then she made me clean the stairs!"

On a mattress on the floor, Tatiana sucked fingers, raw from scouring pans. Sonya, skin boiled red from washday, lay flat on her back beside her. Petra, still heavy with cold, was wrapped in moth-eaten blankets, sniffing and snuffling her way through a mountain of mending.

"Please stop pacing, dear," begged Sonya. "You're making me dizzy."

"She was meant to look after us! *Kind and good*, Mama said!"

"At least she feeds us," wheezed Petra. "All that soup!"

There was a pause while they thought, glumly, about the soup.

"And Mama and Papa will be here soon," Petra went on.

"Ormyirday," mumbled Tatiana, still sucking her fingers.

"Exactly!" said Petra. "On your birthday! Then everything will be lovely again."

Anya threw herself on the mattress and pulled a blanket over her head.

Later, in the bathroom, she scowled at her reflection in Mama's mirror, hanging on a nail above the basin. She looked gray, like the city. They *all* looked gray, even boiled-red Sonya. She picked the mirror off its nail and snapped it shut. A lump rose to her throat as she traced the flowers on its casing. She remembered their first day in the City of Lights, her dream of the white-and-gold drawing room at home. . . .

Other flowers, pink and blue, the name of a square . . .

Oh, *Mama*!

She opened the mirror again and gazed once more at her face.

There must be more to the city than this!

She was a princess.

She was a princess.

She had to do *something*.

࿉ * ࿉

At home, Anya had never been allowed into the street alone.

Princesses don't. She imagined Mama's voice as she slipped out of the house early the following morning. But Mama wasn't here, and Anya now knew Mama made mistakes, because just look at the duchess! Besides, the old rules couldn't possibly apply now that she'd escaped unaccompanied across half a continent and spent her whole time scrubbing.

It had rained in the night. The air was damp and cold. Anya pulled her coat tight around her shoulders and walked fast to warm up, taking long, very unprincess-like strides. Quickly, she came to a crossroads and asked a stranger for directions. In all the time she had been here, she had never used the city's language,

painstakingly learned in the schoolroom at home. The words felt clumsy on her tongue, but to her amazement the stranger understood and pointed.

She hurried on, feeling taller.

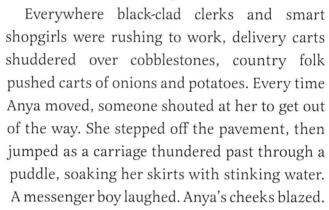

Everywhere black-clad clerks and smart shopgirls were rushing to work, delivery carts shuddered over cobblestones, country folk pushed carts of onions and potatoes. Every time Anya moved, someone shouted at her to get out of the way. She stepped off the pavement, then jumped as a carriage thundered past through a puddle, soaking her skirts with stinking water. A messenger boy laughed. Anya's cheeks blazed.

I am a princess.

I am a princess.

I am a *princess*.

An hour after leaving the duchess's house, Anya stood on the big square with the bare trees and the fountain, frowning at a shop window.

The place with the flowers was a baker's shop. That was all. A completely

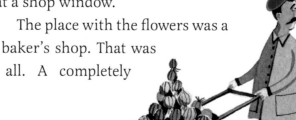

ordinary baker's shop. And there weren't even flowers there anymore. And definitely no magic.

She was so tired, and so cold in her wet clothes. She leaned her forehead against the glass. If she could only rest before the long walk back. . . .

She pushed the door to see if it would open.

It did.

Home slammed into her as soon as she walked in. The air in the shop was warm and sweet. Anya took a breath and tasted butter with cherry jam, felt the soft silk of Mama's dressing gown, the brush of Papa's beard as he kissed her, heard their voices and the cheerful crackle of a morning fire. . . .

Something moved. As fast as it had come, the magic pulled away.

A rat sat on the counter, nibbling a cake.

A cake!

Anya's tummy rumbled. There was a crate of eggs on a table by the door. She reached out, never taking her eyes off the rat.

Take that, rat! And that, and that, and that!

Bam! Crack! Splat! Eggs flew through the air like hard-packed snowballs, spattering the counter like bullets. The rat fled, dropping the cake. Anya pounced and crammed it into her mouth. Almonds and sugar, butter and orange flower exploded on her tongue, spring blossom and country picnics and . . .

"What is going on?"

Cheeks bulging, Anya froze. A man stood in the doorway. Not a man—a *giant*, with a sack of flour on each shoulder, blocking the light from outside.

The baker!

He stared. Anya glanced at the counter, dripping eggs.

"Ah," she said.

The baker folded his arms.

I am a princess.
I am a princess.
I am a princess.

Anya stood as tall as she could—which wasn't *very* tall, compared to the baker—and stuck her nose in the air.

"There was a rat," she announced. "Eating this!" She brandished the cake. "You're lucky I frightened it away."

The baker's eyes flicked to the cake, now missing a princess-sized bite as well as rat nibbles. He held out his hand.

"Oh!" Anya clutched the cake tighter. "Can't I keep it? As a . . . as a reward?"

The baker pushed past her to rummage behind the counter and returned with a square tin box. Anya's mind whirled.

What was in the box?

A gun? A knife? Handcuffs, to arrest her?

He shoved the tin toward her.

"Take one. They're broken, but no rat's been at 'em. Go on, take one, then clear off."

Cautiously, she stood on tiptoe to peer into the tin, and saw that it was full to the top with broken biscuits. Her mouth watered. Her hand inched forward. Then, very politely . . .

"May I take some for my sisters?"

The baker frowned.

"How many sisters do you have?"

She held up three fingers.

"Parents?"

"They're coming soon," she said in a small voice.

The baker frowned again. It was a big frown, which took up his whole face. Anya stared at the floor and hoped that he wasn't about to call the police.

"I need a good rat catcher," the baker said. "If you need a job."

A job! Did princesses *have* jobs? What would Mama say?

"I'd pay you."

"How much?" she asked.

The baker named his sum. Anya smiled and held out her hand.

She had no idea if princesses shook hands with bakers, but she didn't care.

A paid job was a hundred times better than cleaning the duchess's house for nothing.

⌒ ∗ ⌒

The baker, whose name was André, gave Anya the tin of broken biscuits to take home. The sisters ate them after their evening soup, all squeezed up together on the mattress, and Tatiana said they tasted of feather pillows, and Sonya said they tasted of parties. The crumbs made Petra cough, but after she'd recovered she told them a huge, marvelous story about a brave princess who tamed a dragon with cake, and they laughed and laughed for the first time in forever.

It was Petra who insisted that they share with the old people in the house.

"Why?" demanded Anya. "What have they ever done for us?"

"Yes, why?" echoed Tatiana, her hand creeping back to the tin.

But Sonya said Petra was right. And so the princesses went downstairs and offered broken biscuits to old Prince Vasily, who said thank you very much, and to the Countess Kaplinska who cried even more than usual, and to Baroness Maranova, who laughed like a little girl and got crumbs all over her bed.

And that was how the second magic started.

The next day, when Anya arrived home from work, carrying two scorched loaves and three apple turnovers André claimed he couldn't sell, she heard Petra's voice, coming from the kitchen. Running down to show off her treasures, she found her sister on the kitchen table, telling her dragon story to Baroness Maranova, who stood at the stove stirring a steaming copper pan full of twigs.

"Chamomile, rosemary, lavender, mint!" said the baroness. "Our old nurse used to make it for us whenever we were

ill. I found them in the garden, hiding in the ivy and nettles!"

"I think she got up to look for more biscuits," Petra whispered. "But then she heard me cough, and she's been ever so kind."

"She sent Sonya to pawn her watch and used the money to buy a jar of honey, and she's going to make Petra better!" Tatiana was sitting cross-legged under the table with an enormous book on her lap. "I'm learning to read," she whispered. "But I'm hiding in case the duchess finds me and makes me scrub again."

The door swung open, and the prince limped in, shakier than ever because he was only using one stick and carrying a pile of books.

"I knew I was right to bring them from home! Everyone said I was crazy! *Leave the books, Vasily*, they said. *Take diamonds instead*. But see how useful they will be! From now on, Princess Anya, I shall be taking care of your education."

"My education?" stammered Anya.

"Not only yours," said Petra. "Ours too."

"Mathematics!" said the prince. "Philosophy, history, and literature! And reading, for the child! What do you think of that?"

Anya wasn't sure what she thought of that. She had just gotten a job. Must she have an education as well?

"Tea's ready!" called the baroness. "Drink this, Petra, dear. It will go splendidly with your sister's pastries."

The apple turnovers tasted of holidays and hugs. The tea tasted—well, the tea tasted of twigs. "But *nice* twigs," Tatiana said, "and look, Petra's not coughing!"

Sonya dragged herself in from the laundry, took one bite of pastry, and sighed happily that Mama had been right—it *did* melt in the mouth. The Countess Kaplinska, hearing the noise, came downstairs and ate and cried, then amazed everyone by bursting into song.

The duchess had refused the biscuits the evening before, and she refused the apple turnover now. But when Anya toasted the bread and spread it with some of Petra's honey, the tiredness that followed her everywhere finally lifted, and she smiled.

"It tastes of how home used to be," she said. "And do you know, I *do* remember the day your mama and I dug that mirror out of a snowdrift, and how happy we both were to find it! I remember it perfectly."

ᘓᗒ * ᘓᗒ

Spring came to the City of Lights, and the streets began to lose their gray. The plane trees in the fountain square came into leaf, and outside the bakery André planted bright red geraniums. In the garden of the old house, Baroness Maranova discovered currant bushes. Anya found a rusty lawnmower and, after a lot of fighting, worked out how to cut the grass. When it was almost (but never quite) even, Sonya dusted down some old deck chairs and set them in a circle on the lawn where, on fine afternoons, Petra, the baroness, and the countess worked together on the mending they were taking in now for money.

Every morning, Petra and Tatiana took lessons with the prince. Every evening, when Sonya had finished her chores and Anya was back from the bakery, they did *their* lessons.

New foods began to appear in the soup, like beans and even bacon. One Sunday, there were sausages. Sometimes there were eggs.

Tatiana, exploring the attics, uncovered a piano. André brought his brothers to carry it downstairs. Sonya began to play again.

André's sister brought her daughter, Camille, for Sonya to teach.

Camille told her friends about the piano teacher who was also a princess, and soon Sonya was teaching

every day. She used her wages to pay for a doctor for Petra, and a chicken to roast, and new shoes for her sisters. Ugly shoes, they agreed, not like their satin slippers of old, but at least they didn't *pinch*, or let in water when it rained, and that was all that really mattered, even for princesses.

Summer arrived, bringing butterflies to the garden, and Sunday outings to the river, sunburned skin and picnics and paddling, and Tatiana's birthday. . . .

They celebrated it well. Sonya played the piano. André and his brothers and sister-in-law and her daughter sang in their language. The refugees sang in theirs, and then they sang in each other's languages. André, under instruction from Baroness Maranova, had baked a honey cake filled with cream. His sister brought a miraculous pie filled with meat and gravy, and after they had stuffed their faces, they lay about in the garden complaining that their tummies hurt, and it was wonderful.

But Mama and Papa did not come.

Tatiana cried when her sisters took her to bed.

Petra made up a story for her about polar bears and icebergs and Mama and Papa riding across the snow in a dog sleigh.

Sonya sang her a song.

Anya cuddled her.

When she was sleeping, they cried too.

But after another winter and spring and summer, when Petra's cough was a distant memory and Tatiana could read on her own, a letter came. And a few weeks later, another. And a few months after that, when the butterflies were gone again and the leaves had fallen from the plane trees but the old city somehow did not look gray, the bell rang early one morning when no one was expecting it and Sonya, Anya, Petra, and Tatiana ran to open the gates, and Mama somehow gathered all four of her daughters in her arms, and told them they were the most perfect of perfect princesses.

And the mirror? Sonya kept it
and took it with her when she
married and left her family to
live in another city, in a different
country. She gave it to her daughter,
who gave it to hers, who never
knew how it had once saved her
grandmother and great-aunts, and
sold it at a yard sale.

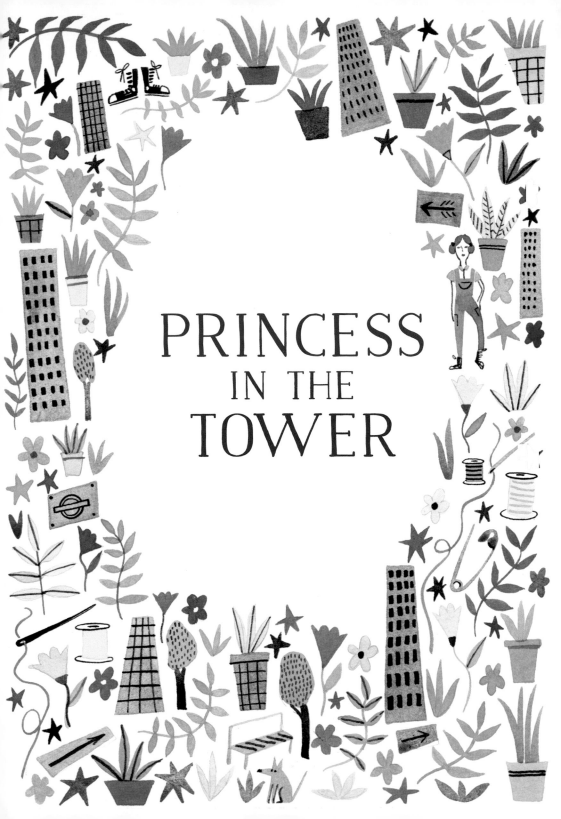

PRINCESS
IN THE
TOWER

PRINCESS IN THE TOWER

O nce upon a time, in a vast city, between a tower block and a railway line, there lay a magical place called the Horace B. Rivers Memorial Garden.

It was not magical in the usual way. There were no elves, no fairies peeping from flowers, no lurking witches. This garden had magic of a different kind.

Horace B. Rivers the man had been married to Grandma Lisbeth, who lived on the thirteenth floor. She was not really a grandma, but everyone called her that because she was kind, bossy, and good at hugs and stories. Grandma Lisbeth adored her husband, and when he died she stopped bustling about telling people what to do and shut herself away in her apartment to mourn. For a long time, her neighbors sat with her, brought her food, and cleaned her home, but after a year had passed and she still wouldn't come out, they decided they had to do more to cheer her up. So Stan from the fourth floor, and Mr. and Mrs. Bata from the seventh, and Khadija and Ali from the eighth, and Ian from the fourteenth, and lots more besides, crowded into René and Zahra's apartment on the twelfth to think. And as they were thinking, Senhora Bel from the eleventh happened to look out of the window at the chestnut tree that stood in the wasteland between the tower and the railway line and said how lonely it looked, and Mrs. Bata said what a shame there weren't more trees to keep it company, and Zahra shouted, "I know! Let's write to the council and ask for permission to turn the wasteland into a garden!"

Everyone looked baffled.

"A memorial garden," Zarah explained. "Where Grandma Lisbeth can look after living things and remember Horace."

They wrote to the council immediately.

The council never wrote back.

After several weeks of waiting, Senhora Bel said, "You know, in my country, nobody ever bothers to ask permission."

So, feeling daring because they were possibly breaking the law, the neighbors went ahead and planted the garden. Stan, who was a builder, cleared some land, while Zahra and René and the Kowalcyks sowed grass and bought as many plants as they could afford, and on a blustery spring morning when everything was ready Khadija and Senhora Bel brought Grandma Lisbeth downstairs to where all her friends and neighbors were waiting to unveil a shiny plaque that read: *The Horace B. Rivers Memorial Garden*. And after everyone had cried and sung Horace's favorite song and eaten Horace's favorite cake, Grandma Lisbeth inspected the garden and announced that they had planted everything all wrong, and she could see

she had a lot of work to do, and everyone laughed because it was so good to have her back.

Over the years, the Horace B grew. Under Grandma Lisbeth's directions, the neighbors planted seeds that turned into flowers, and saplings that grew into trees. They dug flowerbeds and a frog pond, they claimed more land for a vegetable patch, they added a sandpit and swings and benches, a bower for shade, a barbecue for parties. Children played there after school, couples lingered, holding hands, friends worked side by side and gossiped. The garden was a place born of love, Grandma Lisbeth said. A place that looked after its own, where friendships were tended alongside plants, and *that* is what made it magical.

It was the perfect place for Princess to run to when everything went wrong.

ᘛ) * (ᘚ

Princess.

Some said the name started with her dad, René, shouting, "Where's my baby princess?" when he came in from work off the trains. Others said it was because of Zahra, who was a tailor and dressed her from the start in bright homemade dresses, which caused Grandma Lisbeth to coo, whenever she saw her, "My, oh, my, isn't she just like a little princess?" However it started, the name spread. By her first birthday, everyone in the tower called her Princess, and because she was best friends with Stan's daughter, Katy, and the Batas' daughter, Safiye, and Khadija's son, Karim, when they all went to nursery together, everyone *there* called her Princess too, even the teachers. The same happened at primary school.

As the name stuck, so did the clothes.

Zahra taught her daughter to sew, and as she grew up Princess's favorite thing in the whole world was to make new clothes out of hand-me-downs.

"It feels friendlier like this," she explained, when Zahra offered to buy her new fabric. "Like being wrapped in stories."

She made a flowery orange-and-green top out of a shawl of Senhora Bel's that made her feel like a bird of paradise, and she unraveled and reknitted a purple sweater of Ian's into a trailing scarf that made her feel like a film star. Best of all, she cut a pink summer dress from an old dressing gown of Grandma Lisbeth's, with a boat neckline and skirts filled out with layers of tulle from Katy's old ballet tutus. *That* one made her feel as if she was Queen of the World.

The clothes were colorful and strange, but no one laughed at her or said how odd she looked because, well, she didn't. She looked like Princess, and that was a wonderful thing.

But then, in the summer between primary and secondary school, everything changed.

It was supposed to be like every summer, the four of them together—Princess, Katy, Safiye, and Karim. They were going to build a treehouse. Stan was going to take them camping, Zahra and René to the sea. But then the Batas sent Safiye to her grandparents, far away in a different country, and Karim went skateboard mad, and Katy made a new friend at her ballet class called Melody.

Melody didn't live in a tower block but in a big house near the new shopping mall. She didn't like treehouses, or camping, and she only liked the beach if she had to travel on a plane to get there, but Katy thought she was the best thing ever. All she could talk about was Melody's clothes and Melody's phone and Melody's new haircut, until one day, with an embarrassed laugh, she told Princess, "Melody says you can't dress like that now that we're going to secondary school." Princess asked what Katy meant, and Katy in tears said Melody thought Princess was a show-off, and please couldn't she dress normally so they could all be friends? And Princess shouted, "Oh, why don't you just *marry* Melody if you think she's so amazing?"

Grandma Lisbeth was picking slugs one by one out of a strawberry bed when Princess stormed into the Horace B, kicked the chestnut tree, and burst into tears.

"Someone's in a mood," said Grandma Lisbeth.

"I hate stupid ballet!" Princess sobbed. "Also, should I change my clothes?"

"Help me with these slugs," said Grandma Lisbeth. "Then we can eat some strawberries."

And so the garden kept on giving.

People come and people go, but plants and trees stay true. All through the first three weeks of the summer holiday, Princess worked in the garden—planting and pruning, digging and weeding, doing whatever she was ordered to, until Grandma Lisbeth said she had never known the garden so beautiful, and her chest swelled with pride. She was helping to make something even more lovely than the tutu dress, the bird top, the movie-star scarf—something breathing and alive that would last forever. She had always loved the Horace B, but she had never before realized how special it was to how many people—like the new couple on the sixteenth floor, who did tae kwon do there before work, and Susi from the eleventh, who lay in the shade with her baby after breakfast to watch the swooping, swirling swifts, and Mr. Williams from the ninth, who sat in the bower in his wheelchair after lunch to do the crossword.

A month to the day after her argument with Katy, in the summer when everything changed, Princess was drinking tea with Grandma Lisbeth on their favorite bench and thinking about how, although she still missed her friends, it didn't hurt as much.

"You're right," she said. "The garden does look after people. It's like a perfect world, where everyone gets what they need."

"I am always right." Grandma Lisbeth was rummaging in her gardening bag. "Oh, where did I put— aha!"

She pressed something small and round into Princess's hand. "A present for you—a mirror! So next time someone tells you to change, you can look at yourself and remember that you are wonderful!"

"I . . . " Princess didn't know what to say. The mirror was gold and not very shiny, a bit bashed and obviously very old. She traced her finger along the flower engravings on its casing and felt a sudden rush of love—for it, for Grandma Lisbeth, for the garden. "Thank you. It's beautiful."

"Ah, it's only an old thing from a yard sale!" said Grandma Lisbeth, but she looked pleased. "Now, who is this fellow, do you think, sauntering up so important in a suit and tie on this lovely hot day? Look, Princess, he's nailing a notice to the gate—go and see what it says."

Princess got up to look, and her blood froze as she read.

The council had noticed the garden at last

and were planning to turn it into a parking garage for the new shopping mall.

∞ * ∞

All the neighbors crammed into Princess's flat, everyone talking at once.

"They can't steal my Horace's garden!" cried Grandma Lisbeth. "I won't let them!"

"They're not stealing," sighed René. "That's the problem. It's their land. They can do whatever they want with it."

"We must be able to stop them!" cried Princess.

"You can never stop cities when money is involved," hissed Senhora Bel.

"Then we'll make money too!" insisted Princess. "We can fundraise, like we did at school when we needed new books for the library. We can bake cakes. I can make things."

"Oh, Princess!" sighed Zahra. "This is bigger than books and baking or making baby dresses. We need *millions*. . . ."

"We have to *try*, at least!"

"Princess, please."

"I can't believe you're giving up!"

Princess ran out of the room before they could see her cry, then tumbled all the way down the stairs, through the back door, and past the bins to where the Horace B lay, casting long shadows in the evening light. Suddenly, she wished the others were with her. But Safiye was still away, and Karim was off skateboarding, and Katy was somewhere with Melody. . . . Her chest tightened. She longed to go into the garden but it hurt too much to imagine it not being there. Instead, she turned her back on it and started walking. She didn't stop until she reached the station where the music pulled her in.

At first Princess couldn't believe her eyes.

An old homeless woman with matted white hair, dressed in rags shiny with age, and with newspapers tied around her feet, sat at an abandoned piano by the ticket barrier, swaying as she played.

A train came in. Passengers appeared on the steps from the platform and walked past without even looking. Was Princess dreaming? She stepped closer and gagged. *Not* dreaming, no. The old woman stank.

But the music . . .

The music was slow and soft and made her feel

sad, but in a good way. Not the awful, angry sadness she had felt after fighting with Katy—more like the sadness at the end of a good story.

The tempo changed. Now the music was light and bubbling, and Princess closed her eyes as her heart rose with the notes, out of the station to dance with the swifts. . . .

She smiled.

"That's better," croaked a voice. The old woman had stopped playing and was watching her. "Nice threads."

Princess looked down at her gardening outfit,

a bright yellow, flower-patterned jumpsuit, cut down from a sari once owned by Mrs. Reddy from the second floor.

"You don't think it's a bit show-offy?"

"And what is wrong with show-offy, may I ask? A lot of good it would do the world if no one ever showed off! Imagine if I played like this"—the old woman tapped out a few timid notes—"instead of the way I do! I should never get paid!"

She stared pointedly at a basket on top of the piano, filled to the brim with coins.

Princess frowned. How, when not a single passenger had stopped to listen, was the basket full?

She rummaged in a pocket and emptied all the money she had into the basket.

The old woman sniffed. Without much hope, Princess delved into another pocket.

Oh.

Very quickly, before she could change her mind, she added her new mirror to the coins.

"Well!" For a moment, as the old woman stared, it seemed to Princess that she didn't look quite so old, or dirty, or that she even smelled so bad. "Well, well, *well*."

"I didn't steal it, if that's what you're thinking!"

"Oh, I know you didn't!" the old woman said. "Things like this *can't* be stolen. The universe will bless you for this, my dear. Goodness, is that the time?"

"Excuse me?" Princess glanced at the station clock.

When she looked back again, the old woman was gone.

෧ ∗ ෧

From then on, things got strange.

Katy and Karim were waiting for Princess by the entrance to the garden, both looking glum.

"I told Melody about the Horace B!" Katy wailed, her face blotchy from crying. "And she laughed! She's

horrible, Princess! Not like a real friend at all!"

"My board smashed," Karim grumbled. "And I can't afford another one."

Katy's phone pinged. "Safiye's coming home! Tomorrow! Oh, there's another message, I missed it, at seven-thirty—she says she's homesick ..." Katy frowned. "Seven-thirty. That's when I left Melody's ..."

"It's the time I fell off my board," said Karim.

Princess's heart missed a beat.

Seven-thirty—the time on the station clock when the old woman disappeared.

"How strange," Katy said. "But, oh, how good that we'll be together again! Everything back to normal."

She hugged Princess. "I'm sorry," she said. "I was horrible. I love you."

"I'm sorry too," said Karim. "I mean, I don't think I was horrible. But I'm sorry I haven't been around."

Together, they went into the garden and lay on the grass in the darkening twilight.

Everything back to normal, thought Princess. Except it wasn't, was it? Because the notice was still there, nailed to the gate.

And she had thought a garden could last forever!

The liquid-gold notes of a bird spilled into the air, and that was strange too because she had never heard it before.

"It's like music," sighed Karim, and when had Karim ever noticed a bird?

"Like magic," breathed Katy. "Like magic music."

Princess's idea shot through her like a lightning bolt.

She knew exactly what to do to save the garden.

"You want to find an old homeless woman and ask her to play in a concert?" Katy's eyes couldn't have been any wider.

I think it's a lovely idea, wrote Safiye when they messaged her. *But how?*

"We need *millions*," said Karim. "And also a piano. And a *concert hall*."

"There's a piano at the station," said Princess.

"But, Princess, you *can't*," said Katy. "We're children. Grown-ups never pay attention to us."

Princess jumped to her feet and smoothed down her jumpsuit.

"I love you too, Katy," she said. "But you really, *really* have to stop telling me what I can't do. Will you help, or will I do this alone? Because I am *not* giving up without a fight!"

"I'll help!" Karim punched the air. "Seeing as I can't skateboard."

"Katy?"

A tiny nod. Princess hugged her.

"We'll start first thing tomorrow."

჻ ✳ ჻

But the old woman had disappeared.

The four friends looked for her everywhere. In shop doorways and alleyways, on park benches and under bridges, in churches and hostels and hospitals. They

took turns to keep watch at the station.

She was nowhere to be found, and meanwhile the builders had arrived. Men in hard hats marched around the Horace B, measuring out the ground in strips of orange plastic. They circled the old chestnut tree, pointing at which branches to bring down first.

The children resisted the urge to throw things at them from the tower block.

On the day before the diggers were due to start, when all hope seemed lost, the old woman turned up exactly where they needed her, at the piano in the station, dirtier and smellier than ever.

"There you are!" she said to Princess. "I did wonder when you would turn up."

"When *I* would turn up?"

The old woman's fingers drifted lazily over the keys.

"I believe you need my help?"

"How do you—"

"Six o'clock, I think. That's when it's

busiest around here, and I've already cleared it with the station manager. You'll need chairs, to make it feel like a real concert. And bunting—I adore bunting! Mainly, though, you will need an audience, so I suggest you run along and spread the word as quickly as possible."

"If you knew we needed you, why didn't you turn up sooner?" Katy had been staring at the old woman as if she wasn't sure whether to pinch her nose or stamp her foot. "The builders are starting tomorrow!"

"Oh, the universe save us from disbelievers!" For a brief moment, the old woman looked immensely tall and rather scary.

"So you'll play?" Princess asked.

"Naturally." The old woman inclined her head, like a queen. "I owe you a great debt. As show-offy as you can today, Princess, while you spread the word! The pink tulle, I think—you have to show you mean business!"

"What do you mean, a great debt? And how do you know my name? And that I have a pink—"

But the old woman was playing again and ignored her.

All day, the four friends ran backward and forward from home to the station, bringing chairs and benches, spreading news of the concert. Senhora Bel provided multicolored bunting. Grandma Lisbeth cut a bunch of flowers from the garden, saying, "I prefer flowers in the ground where they belong, but this will be like having my Horace with me."

And the afternoon passed, and little by little the station was transformed.

As the time of the concert drew near, Princess began to feel sick.

"What if nobody comes?"

"Of course people will come," said Safiye.

"We need *millions*."

Katy squeezed her hand but said nothing.

Millions felt like an awful lot.

Five o'clock came and Princess's heart thumped as she changed into her pink dress . . . five-fifteen and they headed for the station . . . five-thirty, and people started to arrive.

Five-forty-five and Princess's heart thumped even louder as the crowd swelled.

Five-fifty-five, and she couldn't keep still.

"Where *is* she?"

"She'll come!" said Safiye uncertainly.

"She owes you a *debt*," said Karim, but none of them had a clue what that meant.

Six o'clock came.

Princess's stomach twisted into knots.

Then there was a smell . . . the crowd muttered in surprise as the old lady shuffled in . . . and the music started.

ᑫᑐ＊ᑫᑐ

None of the hundreds of people who were there that evening could quite remember next day what had happened.

There had been a concert of sorts at the station, and a pianist—an old woman, some said, though others claimed that she was young. And the music! On *that* they all agreed. The most joyful music you ever heard—like birdsong, or the rustling of leaves, like wind chimes and the hum of bees. Every person who heard it imagined themselves in a garden, with the cares of the city lifted from their shoulders.

Afterward, someone had cried—a girl in a pink dress, some said, though others claimed she was a princess. Something to do with ticket sales, and millions, and there not being enough, even though the station was packed, with passengers crowding the platforms and people listening all the way down the street. But the truly astonishing thing was what happened when people from the tower blocks along the railway line said *they* wanted gardens like the Horace B.

"Imagine!" they said. "Gardens, gardens, gardens, right to the heart of the city!"

And the council official responsible for parking garages sighed, "Imagine!"

And then a builder called Stan said he would dig them, and a kind bossy elderly lady said she would oversee the planting, and the council official shouted, "I say NO to parking garages!" then produced a contract from her briefcase, ripped it in half, and threw it on the floor and danced on it. And when everyone else understood that the Horace B was saved, and that many more gardens were to be planted, they danced too, including the girl in pink who was perhaps also a princess.

No one quite knew what happened to the pianist. Some said she went up to the platform to catch a train. Others that she walked into the street. One boy swore that he saw the air around her shimmer and that a tall woman with a small gold object in her hand took her place before disappearing into thin air.

But none of the grown-ups listened to him, because what do children know?

THE
MAGIC MIRROR
AND THE
ENCHANTRESS

I am dented!" The mirror, full-sized once more and back on the wall of the library, was not happy. "I am dull! Above all, I am very, very tired and *when have you ever heard of a mirror being tired?*"

The enchantress, reclining on a chaise longue, had the good manners to look embarrassed.

"It wasn't my *best* plan," she admitted. "It never occurred to me that you might get lost. A merry dance I've had, believe me, searching up and down the centuries, all over the world!"

"A merry dance *you've* had?" The mirror's surface flickered. "Were *you* dropped in the burning desert? Did *you* languish in the depths of the oceans? Were *you* swallowed by a giant lizard? Did *you* freeze in the snow? *Were you sold at a yard sale?* I always *said* you were too busy. I always said it would lead to disaster!"

"Poor Mirror! But how fine you look, despite your misadventures!" The enchantress wondered how long the complaining was going to last. Time moved differently in the enchanted palace. It was the night before her goddaughter's naming day, and she was no closer to knowing how to help her be an excellent princess. "Tell me, what have you learned?"

"That the world is cold. And hot. And sandy. And slimy. And cruel. And . . . "

"About princesses, Mirror, dear."

"Oh, *princesses*!"

"That *was* the understanding."

The mirror glowered, as if to remind the enchantress that she may have understood this, but that *it* had had no say in the matter.

"Best of mirrors, you shall have the softest of cloths to clean you, the finest of brushes, the purest of soap and water . . . "

"Stubborn!" the mirror snapped. "Princesses are *stubborn* and proud and bossy, and they do not have very clean fingernails and they are often quite rude, and they are always dashing about rescuing animals or getting into fights or repairing lawnmowers, and they are not remotely interested in lessons."

The mirror paused. Had it been unfair?

"Héloïse was a good student," it conceded. "And it's possible that Leila started to pay attention to her mother's lessons, because she wanted very much to become a good queen, and the laws of her country were rather complicated. And Abayome did get appallingly dirty but then she had to, to rescue Odé, and I know Rose broke that boy's collarbone but she was *extremely* kind to animals. And it *wasn't* fair that Ellen wasn't allowed to sail, and Tica couldn't have saved Choro without being a *little* bossy, and those poor sisters had *nothing* when they arrived in the City of Lights, and as for Princess . . . "

The enchantress leaned forward. "Sweetest of mirrors, I do believe you're turning *pink*! What about Princess?"

"I am certainly *not* turning pink," said the mirror. "It is a trick of the light."

"Tell me about Princess."

"She was not a *real* princess," the mirror said. "It was only a name they called her. Yet she was not so different from the others. They were all . . . "

"Bossy and stubborn and proud?"

"Brave!" The mirror was flickering again. "Brave and fierce and loyal, with big dreams, and even bigger hearts, and such a thirst for the world, and so much love, and . . . "

"Mirror, are you crying?"

"Certainly not! I am a mirror! A mirror never becomes emotionally involved! Imagine the *chaos* if I had *feelings*! I am simply saying that *my* princesses were not excellent because their godmother was an enchantress. They were excellent in themselves. They were excellent *people*."

"You *are* crying."

"I am *tired*."

"Sometimes," the enchantress whispered, "I cry too. I cried when I thought I'd lost *you*."

The mirror was silent. She leaned in closer and thought she heard a hiccup. Gently, she kissed the dulled gold frame. Very briefly, the mirror glowed.

"After the naming day, I shall clean you myself," promised the enchantress.

Then all was quiet, except for the soft, unmistakable sound of a snore.